It's so easy to forget who you really are," Jody admitted.

"That's why we're here together." Eric whispered. Because you have a strange way of seeing me that makes me feel at ease. As if you're seeing through me . . . into me. Making some strange connection between us."

Jody caught her breath, her playfulness forgotten. "I felt that from the moment you rescued me, before I even saw you, or knew who you were. I felt, somehow, that I knew you. In my dreams I felt it. It was your touch . . . your . . . " She fumbled for the right word, gave up.

He reached out and took her hand, lifted her palm to his lips and kissed it, his breath warm on her sensitive skin.

She felt a rush of time, a whirl and swirl of years, her whole life so far racing to this moment. Could it be that all those steps from little girl to woman had led her here, to this place, this moment—this man . . . ?

WHAT ARE *LOVESWEPT* ROMANCES?

They are stories of true romance and touching emotion. We believe those two very important ingredients are constants in our highly sensual and very believable stories in the *LOVESWEPT* line. Our goal is to give you, the reader, stories of consistently high quality that may sometimes make you laugh, sometimes make you cry, but are always fresh and creative and contain many delightful surprises within their pages.

Most romance fans read an enormous number of books. Those they truly love, they keep. Others may be traded with friends and soon forgotten. We hope that each *LOVESWEPT* romance will be a treasure—a "keeper." We will always try to publish

LOVE STORIES YOU'LL NEVER FORGET
BY AUTHORS YOU'LL ALWAYS REMEMBER

The Editors

Loveswept ® 617

Adrienne Staff
Pleasure in the Sand

BANTAM BOOKS
NEW YORK • TORONTO • LONDON • SYDNEY • AUCKLAND

PLEASURE IN THE SAND

A Bantam Book / May 1993

*If you would be interested in receiving protective vinyl
covers for your Loveswept books, please write to this
address for information:*

Loveswept
Bantam Books
P.O. Box 985
Hicksville, NY 11802

ISBN 0-553-44252-X

Published simultaneously in the United States and Canada

*Bantam Books are published by Bantam Books, a division of
Bantam Doubleday Dell Publishing Group, Inc. Its trademark,
consisting of the words "Bantam Books" and the portrayal of
a rooster, is Registered in U.S. Patent and Trademark Office
and in other countries. Marca Registrada. Bantam Books,
1540 Broadway, New York, New York 10036.*

PRINTED IN THE UNITED STATES OF AMERICA

OPM   0 9 8 7 6 5 4 3 2 1

For Bruce, my husband,
my lover, my best friend

One

Up and down. Up and down. Rocking slowly, rocking gently. Tipping, tipping back and forth. Sleepy, sleepy . . . warm and sleepy . . .

Mustering a single ounce of energy, Jody Conners slipped one hand over the side of the rubber raft and dangled her fingers in the sun-warmed, sun-dappled water of the Gulf of Mexico. The golden glare made her shut her eyes, and she stayed that way for a while, totally contented, utterly relaxed, her fingers trailing in the water, the sun on her back.

She'd guessed right: A vacation was just what she'd needed, something quiet, peaceful, and uneventful. Already she felt so much better. Perfect, really . . . totally, obliviously perfect. Of course, the two piña coladas she'd had with lunch hadn't hurt a bit either. Nope . . . they'd melted her bones, loosened her muscles, left her feeling wonderfully unattached to reality, just happy to lie here. Rocking, drifting . . .

Ah . . . this was heaven.

With a smile on her lips, eyes still closed, she floated on. She didn't have to look around to know she was in paradise: turquoise sea, golden sand; turquoise sky, golden sun. True, a few hundred yards up the beach sat her motel, with its rows and rows of identical balconies offering Gulf views at just thirty-nine dollars a night, off-season only. A tacky poolside bar. Pizza and burgers on the strip. And enough T-shirt shops to clothe China. But it didn't matter. Here, on her raft, she could be in Hawaii, or Tahiti, the Greek Isles, Majorca . . . worlds away from the chaos and confusion of her life in Orlando.

Back *there* was reality: the hectic, 6:00 A.M. to 6:00 P.M. grind of running a preschool, molding her life to other people's lives: *their* schedules, *their* needs, *their* demands. It was like balancing a set of wooden blocks one on top of the other, higher and higher, each move shakier, more precarious, until there was just one block too many and the whole pile tumbled to the floor in a heap. *She* was at the bottom of that heap. At least that was how it felt: overwhelming, exhausting, a trap she'd gotten caught in. . . .

It was her own damn fault! She'd invested every cent she had, saved and borrowed money both, taken her best friend, Anne, as partner, bought the Hundred Acre Woods. At the beginning it seemed both sensible and exciting: her own preschool, putting her own ideas to work, turning a struggling little business into a success. She'd jumped in with both feet . . . and gone in over her head.

Oh, just the thought made her tired. So she banished it and lay there dreaming on the raft, rocking, rocking, drifting along on the beautiful warm water. . . .

Suddenly, someone was shaking her awake. Someone was shaking the whole bed! They'd pulled her covers off, and she was cold, and mad. She didn't *want* to wake up, but now— the nerve of them!—they were splashing water in her face. "Hey," she yelled, rolling over, "cut it out. Just—"

With a splash and a yelp she fell off the raft and into the water. She was awake instantly, completely.

"Help!" she screamed, sputtering to the surface. "Help!" She grabbed on to the edge of the raft and pulled it close, hugging it tight against her chest. "Okay, okay . . ." she muttered, spitting saltwater and swiping at her eyes with one hand. "I'm fine. Okay. Okay . . . Geez, I must look like an idiot."

Gritting her teeth, she peeked out of one eye, hoping the whole beach was not watching.

Oh God!

The beach was *gone*.

The sand. Her motel. The other motels.

Gone.

She looked around wildly, thinking, I'm turned around, it's over there, praying, Oh, please, let it be over there. But there was *nothing*.

Nothing.

No beach. No motels. No people. Just the oddest, eeriest bushes growing up on skinny legs in the water. Mangroves. Dark and thick, their branches woven together to form an impenetrable wall, like a wall of claws and thorns, the mangroves rose out of the water. If there was a beach there at all—*anything* safe and solid there at all—it was hidden behind the mangroves like a castle in a fairy tale.

She scrambled onto the raft, thinking of sharks and gators only as she pulled her toes out of the water, but that was enough to lend volume to her screams. "*Help! Help!*"

She continued screaming as the raft rocked and drifted south along the coast with the current.

She felt panic closing in. Dipping her arms into the water up to the elbows, she tried to paddle back north. Harder and harder, the muscles aching in her arms and shoulders, all the way across her back. But the water resisted her feeble efforts, carrying her along slowly but steadily deeper and deeper into the mangrove swamp.

"Help!" she screamed, and a gull screamed back from overhead.

Looking up, she realized the sun was playing hide-and-seek with some very gray, very scary-looking clouds. "Oh no," she whimpered, beginning to cry.

The rain started.

First one fat drop, then another, landed on her back, her head, the tip of her nose. The surface of the water started to dance and jump around her in leaps and splashes. Small whitecaps formed on the rising waves. Little waves turned into bigger waves as the wind blew chill across them.

Jody covered her mouth with both hands, too scared now to cry. Then the raft bucked, and she grabbed on to the top edge, pressed herself against the slick, rubbery surface, and held on tight. Up and down, faster and faster, her heart beating twice as fast as it should, right there in her throat, keeping her from crying or screaming.

The rain pelted her sunburned back and legs, stinging painfully. Saltwater sprayed up over the raft, first from one side, then the other. Her face was wet, her eyes on fire, her mouth filling with water every time she gulped for air. Hopelessly, she pressed her face into the hollow of her armpit, feeling for a second her own warmth, and then, mercifully, not feeling anything at all.

Out of the darkness came a light, and a figure, bigger than life, moving as if on a screen. A voice, deep and husky. Hands reaching toward her.

Jody seemed to watch it all from far away, as if she were a remote observer to this . . . this what? A rescue? Is that what this was, coming like a miracle out of the darkness? From a distance she could sense the comforting sound of his voice, the touch of his hands. Such strong, steady movements, calm and reassuring. If she were that girl there on the raft, she'd feel safe now, she thought. Safe and warm in that man's arms, and she should stop trembling. *Stop trembling, girl,* she silently ordered. *It's all right now. He's saved you. You're safe.*

Two

The rain was beating on his head and shoulders, running down his face and chest in cold rivulets. But the man scarcely noticed, utterly mesmerized by the girl he held in his arms.

She seemed so small, so helpless. Eyes closed, wet hair stuck to sunburned cheeks, she lay there in his arms, vulnerable, pretty, unconscious of his gaze, his beating heart. She was no threat now, and he took his time, looking at her in a way he would never be able to again.

Fate plays strange tricks on us, he thought, and a harsh laugh rumbled in his throat.

Who was this woman washed up on these brambly shores? How did she get here? How far had she drifted on that frail rubber raft?

And how had it happened that he and Matthew had chosen just this route by which to come home tonight? How had the boat's light just happened to catch her in its beam? What made him pause and look out into the storm just at that moment when, instead of guiding the boat in through the mangroves, he had followed some impulse and given Matthew the wheel?

There was no explaining it.

Life never made too much sense. That he knew. A man could go crazy trying to figure it out, trying to brave every blow, do the right thing, hang tough.

But in the dark, in this storm, he could stand and look down at her sweet face and pretend that he'd get to know her. Pretend that he'd hold her until she woke, then look into her eyes and see her smile in relief and gratitude. Pretend she'd speak to him and he'd answer, and there would be that sharp, sweet thrill of the unknown followed by hours and days of getting to know each other.

Dream on! he snarled.

Anger made him rough, and he held her out abruptly to Matthew. "Here. Take her. Put her below. Cover her and stay with her. I'll have us at the dock in no time."

"Are you sure? If you'd rather—"

"Do as I ask." He grabbed the wheel, turning the boat toward home. Then, without looking back, he clamped his jaw tight and said, "Sorry, Matthew. Just please do as I ask."

He could hear the other man's steps leading down into the cabin. Then the only sound was the *ping* of rain on canvas and wood, and the far-off roll of thunder. Around him, the darkness fell like a mask. By feel as much as by sight, he guided the boat in through the twisted hedge of mangroves toward home . . . if anyone could call it that.

Behind Jody's closed eyes the movie had played on.

A man—the same man who had appeared out of the darkness—held her tight. His arms were strong, sure. His chest was hard and warm, solid as a rock but perfect to nestle against. His skin smelled musky, warm, tinged with salt and sweat and a trace of spice. She rubbed her cheek against his chest, feeling the brush of thick, springy hair. If she could have moved her fingers, she would have touched him. But of course not. Not in a movie . . . or a dream . . . or whatever this was. Instead, she lay limp as a rag doll in his arms, wet, helpless, but content.

Then, suddenly, he had let her go, handed her off like an unwanted bundle. There was a roar, accompanied by a quick thrust of movement, and fear chased her back into the unfeeling dark.

Three

When Jody woke, it was dawn. Plain ol' every-day dawn. The light was coming in all pink and pearly around the edges of lace curtains. Pale light, pale curtains, pale walls hung with paint-ings. Recognizable things. Real things. Shutters on the windows, thrown open to let in the morning breeze. A night table with a curving art-deco lamp. A lace-edged sheet tucked up under her chin.

By whom?

When?

Where?

With a start she sat up, but regretted it immediately.

Her skin felt like waxed paper left in the oven on high, crinkled, stiff, ready to crack and crum-ble if touched.

"Ow!" she yelped, holding herself absolutely

still. She was afraid to move, afraid to lie down again, but faint with pain. Her skin was on fire. It hurt so much, everywhere, behind her knees, across her back, and up over her shoulders and the back of her neck. Even her hair hurt! Tears gathered on her lower lids, but before they could spill down her cheeks, the door opened.

A woman came in, hurried to the bed, slid an arm gently under her shoulders.

"Shhh," she whispered, her voice like a sip of cool water. "Sshhh. Just lie back, darlin'. Lie back, and Lena will get a cool cloth for your head. Shhh . . . it's just a lucky thing the fellas found you when they did. Now everything will be all right. Shhh . . ."

Jody eased back against the cool sheets, letting her mind rest on the woman's voice. Yes, yes, it would be all right.

"Here you are, darlin', here's a wet cloth. And now I'm going to get you a little sip of papaya juice, and some nice cool cream to put on your back. Don'tcha worry, darlin', it'll be all right. You had a scare, that's all, but you're fine now."

"Whe . . . where am I?" Jody whispered.

"You wouldn't believe me if I told you. So just don'tcha worry 'bout it now. Shhh . . . sleep for a little while. Just sleep."

This time it was the moonlight dancing across her pillow that woke her. She didn't move. She opened her eyes and looked dreamily at what she could see without turning her head. The curtains were lifting and billowing in the breeze, dappled with moonlight. She could almost believe they were fairy spirits waving at her, beckoning and teasing, playful, mischievous little sprites.

And that moon, just floating there, big as a melon, filling the whole sky, the whole room, with a silvery, iridescent light—the kind of light you see over the ocean. And for a second she could almost believe she was on a ship somewhere, like the Owl and the Pussycat gliding across the moonlit sea. But no. There was no sense of movement. No dip and rise, no gentle rocking. No. She was definitely in a bed, in a house, somewhere.

Now *that* was the question: where?

She was not going to move, not yet, so a better look around was out of the question. Instead, she closed her eyes and listened.

There was music. Somewhere, in a room below, classical music was playing. It sounded like the moonlight, liquid and silvery. And there were voices. She could hear them now, low and even, the comfortable murmur of conversation. Lena? Probably. And who? Her husband? A friend?

The sound of footsteps on the stairs made her turn without thinking. "Ow!" She squeezed her eyes shut in pain.

The footsteps stopped outside her door.

Jody wanted to call out, to ask for help, but the pain held her breathless, dizzy. She clung to consciousness by a thread.

The door opened. She sensed more than saw someone there, a dark presence silhouetted by the hallway light. It came closer, causing a stir in the air, a whisper of movement in the moonlight.

Tears of pain blinded her; moonlight and shadows swam in a haze. Then there was the wooden clatter of the shutters being drawn shut, and darkness filled the room.

"Lena?" she breathed, trembling with pain and fear. "Who's there? Who—"

"Shhh," a man whispered. "It's all right. Here, let me hold you. Lean against my shoulder—"

"Yes . . ." she sighed, floating gratefully on the welcome, familiar sound of that deep, husky voice. His shoulder was more comfortable than any pillow, his touch strong yet gentle. "It's *you.* Oh, I'm glad," she whispered, as his cool hand stroked her forehead.

"Ah, my sleeping beauty, rest . . . just rest now."

"Will you stay? I . . . I'm frightened."

"Yes, I'll stay. Just sleep now."

"No. You'll vanish, disappear like my dreams."

"Perhaps this is only a dream. Sleep now. Shhh."

"Wait, hold me . . . don't let go . . . I don't want to sleep. . . ."

But against her will, Jody slid deep into unconsciousness.

When Jody awoke the next morning, she felt the way she did when the headache she'd been nursing all day was suddenly gone. When the sore throat she'd had all week disappeared and she could swallow again. When her toothache was fixed and she could bite into a juicy red apple once more, or that Hershey bar with almonds.

Great! Glad to be alive!

She reconsidered as she tried to swing her legs over the side of the bed. Maybe *not* ready for handstands and high jinks, but if she took it nice and slow, she thought she could make it to the bathroom.

She shuffled in, holding on to the wall and then the rim of the sink. Leaning closer, she squinted at herself in the mirror.

She looked awful. Her hair was full of salt, stiff as straw, standing on end like a broom. Her lips were dry and chapped. Her cheeks and nose were peeling.

Pushing away from the sink, she shuffled to the shower, turned on a fine spray of luke-warm water, stepped out of the nightgown that someone—Lena, and not one of the "fellas," she prayed—had put her in, and edged under the water. She gingerly lifted her arms and lathered her hair. Umm, heavenly.

She didn't want to come out. But finally the water went from warm, to cool, to cold, and she hurried out, patting herself very gently with a soft, fluffy towel.

Then she froze. There was someone in the bedroom. She could hear movement, footsteps, followed by a soft click as the door was closed.

Jody pressed an ear to the bathroom door, straining to hear.

"Lena? Lena, is that you? Is anyone there?"

Wrapping the towel tightly around her, she opened the door a crack and peeked out. "Hello?"

The room was empty.

Except there on the night table was a breakfast tray filled with temptations: a white rose, a small glass of juice, a basket of warm, sweet-smelling muffins, and a plump Victorian teapot, hand-painted with tiny roses and miniature birds. The cup and matching saucer were thin enough to be almost transparent.

She savored breakfast bite by bite, careful not to get crumbs on the beautiful sheets, and then lay half-propped against the downy pillows, sipping tea. There was a knock on the door.

"Are you awake in there? It's Lena."

"Come in, please," Jody called.

"Well, good morning to you, girl. You are surely looking a lot better today."

"I'm feeling a lot better," Jody answered with a smile. "That wonderful breakfast helped. Thank you so much."

"You're more than welcome."

"And let me introduce myself." She rose stiffly and held out her hand. "I'm Jody. Jody Connors."

Lena took the hand in both of hers. "You sit on back down," she said gently. "No standing on ceremony here. Jody . . . hmmmm?" she said, cocking her head to one side. "It suits you. Nice to meet you, Jody. Now all you've got to do is rest and get your strength back."

"I will. But if I put on some clothes and come downstairs, will you tell me where I am and how I got here?"

"No." Lena wagged a finger at her, frowning. "You are not to get out of bed. Those are the orders I was given, and I am passing them on to you. You are to stay in this room. Relax. I'll bring you magazines and books, and I can turn the music on if you would like. And you may go as far as that desk there under the window if you want to write a note and let someone know you are fine—"

"Ohmigosh! I've gotta get up . . . I've gotta call home," Jody gasped, struggling to her feet again.

"Sit . . . yourself . . . back . . . down." Lena punctuated each word with a wag of her finger, then put a restraining hand on Jody's shoulder. "You are one impetuous young woman, which is probably how you ended up in this mess to begin with. Now listen to me. There are no phones here, so no reason to get all in a tizzy. No telephones, no telegraph, no fax machines. You can write a letter if you'd like, and the . . . Matthew will post it this evening by boat."

"By boat? Matthew?" Jody repeated. Each piece of information was more startling than the one before.

"Yes, child. We're on an island—"

"An island?"

"Yes, one of the ten thousand islands up at the northwest corner of the 'glades. Whatever you were doin' out in that ocean alone heaven only knows, girl, but you must have drifted on south with the current away from Marco Island, down on toward Fakahatchee Pass. Lucky for you the current pushed you on into the mangroves; you wouldn't have made it out in open water in that storm. As it is, you got yourself quite a burn, besides being dehydrated and scared near to death. But there's no sense in dwellin' on that. You're here and fine."

"But *where* is *here*? What's the name of this island?"

"It doesn't have a name."

"What do you call it when you talk to other people, to strangers?"

"I don't do much talking to strangers. Not too many folks float in here on the waves. No, I live here with Matthew, my husband, and we've had no need for naming it."

"And just the two of you live here? Alone?"

Lena stood, suddenly thin-lipped and businesslike. "Let me get you some hot tea, Jody—"

"I want answers, not tea! Oh . . . oh, I'm sorry," Jody said, patting the bed. "Please sit back down. I didn't mean to yell. Something about this whole thing just scares me. Tell me everything, please. Where we are, who lives here . . . who that man is I keep seeing in my dreams—"

Lena patted her hand. "There's nothing to be scared of here, child. This is just a private island. A private island with no name, and no address, and the man who owns it likes it that way."

"Is that who found me? That man? Was it him?"

"Why . . . Matthew found you. He was out on the boat—"

"I thought you had said 'the fellas' found me?"

"Fella . . . fellas . . ." Lena shrugged. "It was Matthew—"

"Just Matthew?"

"Now why are you so curious about that, pray tell?"

Jody lifted both shoulders and met Lena's eyes. "I picture a man . . . someone I've seen before . . . familiar . . . someone tall and handsome, strong . . ."

"You could be describin' Matthew."

"Am I?"

"You say you got a good look at this man?"

"No, not at all. It was more a feeling I had, like I was in a dream . . . or, well . . ."

"Yes?"

"Don't laugh, but it was like I was in a movie."

"A movie?" Lena repeated, looking out the window. "What an odd thing to say. But then," she added, turning back and smiling, "you were in a pretty unusual predicament. No tellin' what tricks our minds will play on us." She stood, smoothing the edge of the sheet. "Now you stop worryin' about this an' that and get some sleep. I've got to go make some lunch."

"Wait. Could I meet Matthew? Please?"

"You're supposed to rest—"

"Please, Lena? I'd feel so much better."

Lena gave Jody a quick, appraising look that melted into a sympathetic smile. "Well, child, if it's that important to you, certainly Matthew can make a guest appearance. You just wait here."

She stepped lightly to the bedroom door and called out, her voice singing through the house, "Matthew, come here, man!"

When there was no answer, she called again. "Matthew, where the devil are you?"

"I'm right here, Lena," a man answered, appearing in the bedroom door. He had shoulder-length bushy white hair, which was held back by a bandanna knotted around his forehead. He had an eagle's nose, Jody thought, and dark, leathery skin. He could have been a sixties hippie, a Greek fisherman, or an Indian warrior. But he was *not* the man she had dreamed.

"Well, you're looking a whole lot better," Matthew said.

"Thanks to you." Jody stood up and held out her hand. Her fingers were ice-cold, her hand shaking. She tried to smile, but her head was spinning, and black spots were jumping in front of her eyes.

Lena snapped her fingers. "Introductions are over. Matthew, you help that child back into bed, and I'll bring along some hot tea and biscuits. And, Jody . . . you are not to budge from here all day, understood?"

Jody nodded. But her head was filled with questions. And someone on this island knew all the answers. She just had to find out who he was.

Four

It was close to midnight, but Jody was wide awake, staring into the darkness.

Down below, there were footsteps in the kitchen, a squeak of salt-rusted hinge in the stillness, and then the screen door slammed shut.

Jody hurried to the window and held her breath. A yellow circle of light spilled from the kitchen, but it was empty. Just beyond it were the dark shadows of the thick, junglelike foliage growing almost up to the house itself. Palm trees, vines, hibiscus plants fifteen to twenty feet tall reaching up past her window, banana trees curving downward, heavy with fruit. All the black textured shapes were stirring and moving in the island night. Ten men could have been standing there right below, and she'd never see them.

She raised on tiptoes and pressed her face

closer to the screen. Had *he* come out for a smoke? To take a walk? Watch the stars? Or was he standing there in the shadows that very moment, looking up at her?

With a start she leapt back and pressed herself against the wall. There was something spooky about this whole thing.

Why would someone rescue her, take care of her, but never let himself be seen?

Secrecy? Fear? Maybe he was a wanted man, hiding here, holding Lena and Matthew hostage. Nah. Lena and Matthew seemed happy as pie.

What if there was something terribly wrong with this man? Some dread disease, some hurt, some physical scar.

Drawing a shallow breath, she peeked back out the window.

There he was! A man. Silhouetted in the moonlight. A tall, slim man standing at the water's edge, legs apart, arms crossed over his chest, his hair a bit long and wild, blown by the night wind. Just a dark shape.

But real.

Someone was really there. Who?

Without stopping to think, Jody slipped out of her room, hurried down the stairs, and paused at the kitchen door. Empty—good. She tiptoed through and pulled the door softly closed behind her.

She used the shadows to her own advantage, staying close to the woven trunks of the palms, moving silently beneath the rustling leaves. Every few seconds she'd stop and listen for footsteps coming toward her along the path, but there were none. She moved stealthily through the dark, feeling the crunch of shells and stones, edging slowly down toward the beach. Around a curve, and there it was, the sand spread like a blanket before her in the moonlight, silver sand stretching to the white ruffles of the surf, to the black heronlike legs of the mangroves framing the beach on the right and left, and there— directly ahead, still facing the water—was the man.

A thousand prickles walked her spine, fingers lifting the hair at the back of her neck.

What would happen if she stepped out of the shadows and called to him? Would he run? Would he hide? Would he turn slowly, until he was facing her?

Instead, she stayed hidden, trembling. And he stood motionless, unaware that he was being spied upon.

I should leave, Jody scolded herself. But she remained there, drawn to him, strangely compelled to watch and wait. It was as if there were a hand at her back, pressing her forward.

Up close he was not as tall as she'd imagined, but broader in the shoulders, though his hips were slim, his legs long and lean in his jeans. His hair still blew in the wind and tossed about like an unruly storm, but because moonlight spilled silver on his head, she couldn't tell what color his hair was, just that it was dark and wild.

He moved, and her heart stopped. But he only shifted his stance, shoving his hands into his pockets, scuffing at the sand with one bare foot.

She had to open her mouth to breathe; her heart thumped like a drum.

And as if he did sense something, the man stiffened. Half turning his head as if to peer over his shoulder, he stood listening. Then he shrugged and looked back over the water.

Relieved, Jody let her breath out through parted lips. She'd caught a glimpse of cheek and jaw that certainly seemed human enough, handsome even. Lord, what had she been expecting? Beauty's Beast? The Creature from the Black Lagoon? She had managed to give herself a good scare.

Rubbing her hands up and down her arms, she bit her lip, shivered—

"Who's there?"

Jody gasped and backed away, stumbled, bumped into a palm or a bush, she didn't know what.

"Lena? Matthew? Is that you?"

He turned, held one hand up as if to shade his face from the moonlight. "Who is it? Is someone there?"

Jody froze, not knowing whether to turn and run, or hide and hope not to be found.

"Don't move!" the man shouted. He thrust one hand deep into a pocket and glared in her direction. "Just don't move. I've got a gun here, and I'll blow your head off. I may not be able to see who you are, but I know you're there."

Whatever Jody expected, getting shot was not it. Frantically she yelled out, "Don't! Please don't! I didn't mean—"

"Who the hell—?" The man raked both hands through his hair, then shook his head. "Don't tell me. My houseguest?"

"I'm sorry," Jody whispered. "Really. But you're not going to shoot me, are you?"

"I should! And if I *had* a gun, I just might!" Again he pushed his fingers through his hair, tense, scowling, the hand held there to shade his face.

Relief swept through Jody. She rushed forward, hands out, eager to show herself and prove she was harmless, defenseless.

He leapt back as if *she* were aiming a weapon at *him.*

"It's okay—" she began.

"Stay back!" he shouted.

"But I—"

"Stay back!" He had retreated to the water's edge and stopped there, trapped.

"It's just that you scared me."

"*I* scared *you*?" he repeated, his voice harsh with anger. "What the hell do you think you did, creeping up on me like that? Didn't Lena ask you to stay in your room?"

"But—"

"Didn't she?"

"Yes, but—"

"Was that too much to ask, considering the courtesy we've shown you? That *I've* shown you? Hiding in shadows, walking the beach alone in the middle of the night?"

"But that's what seemed so weird!" she answered quickly, trying to explain, trying to see his face, judge his anger. "I couldn't figure it out—"

"So for curiosity's sake you invaded my privacy?" His voice was cold now. Furious. He took a step toward her.

"I'm sorry," she whispered.

"You should be. Now go back to the house. And stay there." He seemed barely able to contain his anger.

"I will. I'm sorry," she said. "I am. Really." She turned to go, then stopped, looking back down the dark path. "But I didn't see you, if that matters. I mean . . . I couldn't identify you . . . to the police or anything, if that's what you're worried about. Not that I would anyway, I mean—"

"Go!"

"Yes, yes, I'm going." She spun and ran into a tree. For a moment the shock kept her upright, but then she crumpled to her knees.

She heard him curse even as the world spun. "Are you all right?" His hands were on her arms, lifting her up, and then his arms were around her, steadying her against his chest. She could feel his breath on her face.

She knew she shouldn't open her eyes, just pretend she'd fainted and leave it at that. But she couldn't.

She looked up at him.

At Eric Ransom. The movie star who disappeared four, five years ago. Hollywood's gorgeous Bad Boy. Hero and sex symbol, dark and oh-so-desirable Eric Ransom. Looking just the way he did in *The Empty Doorway*, *Run with the Wind*, and *Outcast.* How he had made her cry—and lust—in *Outcast.* And here he was.

And here *she* was!

"Oh my," she said, and fainted dead away.

When she opened her eyes, the bedroom was full of people: Lena, Matthew, a young man wearing jeans and a T-shirt, *and* Eric Ransom.

Jody sat bolt upright. "My head!"

"Serves you right," Ransom muttered.

"Eric," Lena scolded. "Hush now. It's your own fault as much as this girl's. We told you to send her home *two* days ago, when Chandler offered to fly her out. But no, you wouldn't hear a word we said—"

"Nor do I want to now." Eric brought the conversation to a halt by stalking out of the room.

Lena shook her head after him, clucking her tongue. "That man. His own worst enemy—"

"Let him be, Lena," Matthew chided. "We've got enough of a problem right here." He tipped his head toward the bed . . . and Jody.

"Me?" Jody gulped. "I'm no problem, honest," she assured them.

"But you know who he is, where he lives," the young man said, flexing his muscles. He looked as though he could bend an iron bar in half. And wanted to.

"I'd never tell," Jody insisted.

"Sure. With the reporters banging on your door and Hollywood waving exclusives in your face? Ha! I bet!" the boy sneered.

"You can trust me."

"It's not *me* who has to trust you." And then, adding insult to injury, he muttered, "Shoot, this is what comes of being trusting in the first place. Of being nice. I told him, 'Get her out of here, Eric.' But no. You were too hurt to move, and now look who's going to pay for it."

Jody tossed the covers back and climbed out of bed. She marched right up to him, muscles or no muscles. "I said I wouldn't tell, and I won't. Believe me if you want, or don't; I don't care. But it is the truth."

He stared at her.

She stared back.

Matthew broke the deadlock. "It's not up to any of us. It's up to Eric. He's the only one with something to lose."

"What about me?" Jody whispered.

"You?" Matthew snorted. "What have you got to lose, girl? We'll leave you here, then call the Coast Guard when we're safe away. Gone. Without a trace. We've done it before. And you . . . you'll end up with a fancy vacation and a good story to tell."

"You mean he'd just leave? All this? His home?" Jody asked, dismayed.

Her question seemed to kindle Matthew's anger. "He doesn't have much choice now, does he? Which seems like a real shame to me, considering how much he's already gone through. And besides, he's got everything organized from here; it won't be easy running things from Europe, or—"

Lena lifted a warning brow, and Chandler quickly took the cue.

"Come on," he said, heading out the door. "We can talk downstairs. Maybe we can think of something." He turned and pointed a finger at Jody. "*You* stay here!" he ordered.

"The hell I will!" Jody snapped, brushing past him and hurrying down the stairs. "Where is Mr. Ransom? If I could explain to him—"

"You're the last person Eric wants to see right now," Matthew yelled, running after her, Lena and the boy following.

"Hold it!" It was Eric Ransom, standing at the foot of the stairs in pajama bottoms, tying a robe around his waist. "What the hell is going on *now*?"

Jody raced down the stairs and grabbed Ransom's arm. "Listen, they think I'm some danger to you, that you've got to run away, leave your home, do all kinds of things, but I'm not, really I'm not, especially after all the kindness you've shown me."

The boy took one step toward them, but Ransom halted him with an uplifted hand. "Why don't the three of you go on to bed—I'll take care of this."

"But—"

"Good night, Chandler. Good night, you two." He waved Lena and Matthew on to their bedroom. Waited for the stairway to clear. Listened for the sound of doors closing. Then he looked down at Jody. "Okay. You were saying?"

"Can we sit down somewhere?" asked Jody,

already turning toward the living room and a comfortable couch.

"I think not."

She stopped, startled. She thought he had understood, had realized she was on his side. But the air between them was bristling with tension.

"Well?" he demanded.

She looked up at his face. It was the oddest feeling: Here was this total stranger whose face was so well known, so familiar; the rugged jaw, the mouth with its chiseled upper lip and fuller bottom lip, the dark, impenetrable eyes. She wondered what he was really like, what lay beyond the surface beauty that drove him to hide. She tipped her head to look at him better and saw that the color was rising across his face, giving a coppery warmth to his tan skin, saw how the dark skin, dark brows, dark, dark eyes, all worked so well together, giving him a look of strength and vulnerability, especially now, with him blushing like that. It stole her breath.

"Don't do that," he snapped, and turned away.

"What?" Jody asked. "What did I do?"

"Don't look at me like that."

"Like what? I didn't mean anything."

"I hate it."

"I . . . I'm sorry." She shrugged, finding herself at a loss for words.

"Forget it. Go to bed. I'll work everything out in the morning."

She put a hand on his arm, stopping him before he could leave. "There is nothing to work out, Mr. Ransom. I told you that already. You

don't have anything to worry about from me.
You certainly don't have to leave your home, or
run off to Europe or something." She dropped
her hand. "Honest. I will never mention this to
anyone. I'm sorry I followed you to the beach.
I'm sorry I invaded your privacy. It was wrong
of me. And I'm sorry if I embarrassed you now.
I . . . I didn't mean anything by it. You happen
to be a famous man, an exceptionally handsome
famous man, and I never expected to see you in
person."

"And when you meet a *person*, you always
stare at them like that?"

"No, of course not."

"That's what I mean. You weren't looking at
me like a person, but a thing, something to buy,
something to possess—"

"No!"

"No?" he repeated, searching her face.

"You shouldn't be so touchy."

His brows dipped over wary eyes. "I shouldn't,
huh?"

"Nope."

"And what other advice would you give me?"

"I'd tell you to put me on the next boat heading north, and not give me another thought. You
can rest easy."

"I can? You're sure of that?"

"Yup."

He nodded slowly, never taking his eyes from
her face. Then he shrugged. The robe fell open
across his bare chest, showing tan skin and dark
curly hair, broad, supple muscles.

Jody said softly, "And you should bundle on up in sweats or something if you don't want any staring." With effort she pulled her eyes away and back up to his, only to find him giving her the strangest look.

"What?" she whispered.

"I was thinking that you'd better do the same."

She frowned, puzzled. "Me?" Then she dropped her eyes to her cotton shift and blushed herself. "I got used to thinking of myself as the eternal invalid, wasting away in the upstairs tower." She took a step backward, feeling behind her for the banister. "Well, I guess I'll just head back up. It was nice meeting you." She turned around and ran up the stairs.

Behind her door, face muffled in a pillow, she felt mortified. Lordy. She'd just talked to Eric Ransom while dressed only in a borrowed nightie!

Five

Eric stood outside his own kitchen door, lurking in the shadows like some criminal. But he didn't feel like a thief, a burglar. No. He felt like a fool.

He knew better than to risk everything: his safety, his privacy, his sanity. He knew better, from years of experience. From lessons filled with pain and torment and disappointment. He knew better.

But his heart was urging him on. *Open the door*, it said. *Take a chance. One last time take a chance.*

He could hear her voice. It floated from the kitchen like a bird's call, light, airy, innocent, filled with music. It made him furious. "What the hell is she feeling so good about this morning?" he grumbled. The answer came to mock him: *You're jealous. Jealous of her love of life, her honesty, her openness.*

He was just smart. Wise to the world. Tough as steel. He didn't care a bit about her voice, her smile, the softness of her skin, the intelligence in her eyes, the sheer energy of her. He didn't need any of it. Didn't trust any of it. Wasn't foolish enough to want any of it . . . to hope . . . to dream.

Behind him, a heron cried in the mangroves, a loud, piercing call that hung in the morning stillness. Eric rocked back on his heels, shoved his hands deep into his pockets. The muscles across his shoulders and neck ached with tension. His whole body felt taut, stretched tight as a wire, humming with frustration.

The heron cried again. There would be good fishing today. That's what he should do: Take the small boat out among the mangroves and fish. Forget this. Forget it all. *Just turn around, Ransom,* the voice said loud and clear in his head. *Turn around and get out of here. Now!*

What the hell was he waiting for?

What the hell was he hoping for?

Clenching his fists and locking his jaw, he pulled the kitchen door open and stepped inside.

The screen door opened with a squeal, then slapped shut behind him. "Morning," he said.

Jody had been sitting with her back to the door, watching the hallway for any sign of him. His entrance caught her by surprise, and she spun around in her seat. He was *real.* And he was here.

She caught the scowl on Chandler's face, the knowing glances exchanged by Lena and Matthew. She wanted to strangle all three of them. Instead, she rested an arm lazily on the back of her chair. "Good morning," she answered, and gave Eric a smile.

"What's going on here?" he asked, hesitating halfway into his chair.

"Nothing to worry about," Lena insisted, settling him with a hand on his shoulder. "Can I get you some orange juice?"

"No thanks. Coffee's fine. Sit back down."

There were a few minutes of quiet as everyone ate the pancakes Lena had made for breakfast. Then Eric, as if this were any ordinary morning, asked, "So, what's on the schedule for today?"

"I should fly her back. Immediately," Chandler volunteered, pointing a fork in Jody's direction. "I can be ready in an hour."

"An hour," Eric said. His eyes met hers across the table. "What do you say, Jody?"

It was the first time he had said her name, and she felt a sudden thrill, and a strange sense of connectedness. Somehow this seemed like fate. It made her foolish and daring. "I can't possibly be ready in an hour," she said.

"You can't?" he asked, a smile tugging at the corner of his beautiful mouth.

"No, I can't. Absolutely not."

"Why not?"

She took the chance, rushed right in where angels fear to tread. "Because I don't want to. I don't want to leave yet."

The other three were like an audience at some unrehearsed play, where the actors had not yet learned their lines or recognized their cues, and everyone's taken by surprise. Their eyes went from Jody to Eric, as they wondered what would happen next.

He lifted his shoulders, frowning. "I don't blame you. I wouldn't want to leave yet either. It's the kind of place where anything could happen."

"Yes," she answered. "That's the feeling it gives me, too . . . though I've seen very little of it. There seems so much to explore, to learn about. I've seen only the view from my bedroom window. And I haven't even been out on the beach yet."

"Just down the path to the edge of it all."

"Right. And only in the dark."

"Which isn't the right way to see it," he said.

"No, of course not," she agreed.

"And you haven't seen the herons. They nest near here, did you know that?"

"No, but I'd love to see them."

Matthew rolled his eyes and got a swift kick under the table for his trouble. Chandler was stunned.

But Jody was oblivious to them all. She saw only Eric's face, heard behind the words he was saying *other* words: *Stay. Wait. Don't go yet.* She could be making it all up, but she'd take that chance, come what may.

Eric was watching her. No . . . he was studying her, his dark eyes narrowed and intent, his gaze probing. Ignoring the others, he leaned both elbows on the kitchen table, resting his chin on his hands, looking at her. But it was already decided. "I think you'd better stay a day or two. If you can?"

"I can."

"You're sure?"

"Oh yes, I'm quite sure."

"Good." He nodded and pushed his chair back from the table. "Then, if you're finished, why don't you come with me." He held out his hand.

Jody swallowed once, leaned back in her chair. "Give me a moment, will you? Let me find something to put on."

Lena stood, taking coffee cups with her to the sink. "There are some things in the closet in your room. Something there may fit."

"Thank you, Lena," said Jody, standing. She looked at Eric. "Will you wait here?"

"I'll be outside," he replied, and left.

Jody excused herself and walked slowly out of the kitchen, then up the stairs. She couldn't explain her desire to stay, not rationally anyway. She knew only that sometimes you've got to just shoot for the moon.

An odd assortment of clothes were hanging in the closet. Women's clothes. Obviously not Lena's. Well, what had she expected: a monk? This was Eric Ransom.

She took a quick survey that netted her a one-piece jumpsuit and a pair of sandals. She rolled the pant legs up, brushed her hair, and hurried back downstairs. Without a pause she flew through the kitchen. *Don't stop. Don't think,* she cautioned herself. *If it's wrong, I'll take the consequences. If it's right, it could be magic.*

* * *

Eric led Jody down the same path she'd stolen down in moonlight the night before.

Now the sun was beating on their heads and shoulders, warming the gravel and the little lizards who lay on the stones. With a flick of a tail they'd vanish, melting into the shadows cast by the dense foliage. One lone challenger, eight inches long from nose to tail tip, stood his ground; lifting his head, he puffed out his throat sac till it blazed red as fire, a miniature flag; then he, too, turned tail and ran.

At the edge of the sand Eric kicked off his sandals, so Jody followed suit, and they walked barefoot down to the mangroves where the water ebbed and swirled among the dark roots.

He was quiet, withdrawn. Jody gave him time, glad for a chance to catch her own breath.

Then Eric nudged a tall, skinny mangrove with his toe. "I like these things for some reason," he said, half to himself. "Odd, ugly, but mysterious, aren't they? And they keep the world at bay."

"Like the bramble hedge," she answered, "in *Sleeping Beauty*. The one that grew around the castle until the prince appeared?"

His eyes swung back to her face and lingered there, searching, trying to read something in her expression.

"What?" she asked.

"You say the oddest things. I never know what to expect. Where do you get these ideas?"

"Fairy tales," she admitted, then knew she'd

better explain before he really thought she was crazy. "I teach preschool. Three- and four-year olds. Fairy tales are very important. They hold all kinds of truths."

He was listening. Holding her hand now and listening. So there was nothing to do but keep talking.

"Actually, a friend and I own a little preschool on the south side of Orlando. We call it the Hundred Acre Woods . . . from *Winnie-the-Pooh*?"

He nodded. His attention was as focused as a camera's eye, as if he were truly interested in preschool education and had just been waiting for her to stop by to explain it all to him.

"It's nothing like the big franchises you see around. It's modified Montessori, hands-on learning, developmentally appropriate. We stress positive self-concept, success, feeling good about themselves; for us, that's more important than academic preparation. But we're certainly not just baby-sitting. It's lots of love and hugs—"

"I guess that works when you're four."

"It works *all* the time, if you're lucky enough and determined enough to find it." She ducked her head, grinned, and clucked her tongue at her own outspokenness. "Sorry. I tend to get carried away when I really believe in something."

"But you also believe in fairy tales," he said softly.

"No. Yes . . . well, I believe in the message at the heart of fairy tales. The possibility of magic. Don't you?"

"No."

"Not at all?" She tipped her head to see his face better against the sun's glare. She hadn't noticed before, but there were gold flecks in those dark brown eyes, those gorgeous eyes, those Gypsy lover eyes. And when he smiled like that, they narrowed, and crinkle lines fanned around the corners, and—

She broke the gaze. Careful, careful, her inner voice warned. Too fast, too fast. . . .

But when she tried to edge away, he held her hand tight. "I was just about to tell you, you have beautiful eyes, Jody."

"Thank you," she replied, catching at the wispy edges of her composure. "I was going to say the same."

He laughed and shook his dark head. "I never know *what* you're going to say next."

"Neither do I," she admitted, slipping her hand from his and folding her arms across her chest. "It seems to be a habit of mine. For example, you won't believe this, but I bought the Hundred Acre Woods on a dare . . . well, a brag . . . well, *whatever* you call it. I didn't give it a whole lot of forethought and planning. My friend Anne called to say it was up for sale—the owners were filing for bankruptcy, and her husband was handling their books, so he knew about it first—and I said, 'Heck, *we* could do a better job than that.' And the next thing I knew, there I was: co-owner, administrator, teacher, the whole shebang."

"Impetuous."

"Terribly. But I'm working on it."

He lifted his broad shoulders in a shrug. "I don't know if I'm glad to hear that . . . or not."

"I don't want to make the same mistakes twice."

"Neither do I," he answered softly.

In the silence that followed, a gull cried. Another answered, and the two flew off together, white wings flashing in the blue sky.

Eric scuffed at the sand with his bare foot, drawing circles and erasing them as fast. "So . . . besides running a preschool, what do you do?"

"Oh, between teaching and conferences and administration and making nice to the parents and the staff, there isn't time for much else."

"But *what* else? Tell me. Do you play tennis? Ski? Go bowling? Paint? Have a husband, an ex-husband, a lover, a—"

"None of the above. I mean," she explained, counting off on her fingers, "no husband, ex-husband, lover, boyfriend, steady companion. I *do* play tennis, but badly. I love to hike, and I write poetry, and I do needlepoint, and I like to cook Chinese food. I make great spring rolls and siu my, which are dumplings—"

"I know."

"You do? Well, you'll have to taste mine sometime. And what else? Well, I love cats. Dogs. All animals, really. And I love the movies and theater and the ballet, but I fall asleep at operas, and—"

"How old are you?"

"Thirty-one. Just. How old are you?"

He laughed, a flash of white teeth that conjured up a dimple in his left cheek. "I'm thirty-nine. Forty in December."

"Oh, I couldn't remember. I suppose I could have guessed fairly close by thinking back to articles about you."

"It's okay, Jody, it's not one of those important facts you're required to memorize, like when the Magna Carta was signed or D-Day."

Was he teasing? But even though he was still smiling, a shadow had drifted across his eyes. He took a step back. "Let's walk."

"Sure. I'd love to."

He led her up past the high-water mark to where the sand was so warm, it had a crust like the top of a freshly baked cake, soft as flour, crumbling under their bare feet, holding the shape of their footsteps even when they'd moved on.

He lay down on his back, arms folded under his head, then looked up at her. "Join me?"

She didn't hesitate to drop down beside him, pillow her head on her arms, and look up at the sky.

"What do you see?" he asked.

"Clouds flying. Clouds sailing. Mare's tails and cotton puffs. And there, a lion with a ruffly mane, or, wait, a dragon, and those are his silver scales, his clawed foot." She paused, then turned her head toward him. "What about you?"

He didn't answer, and for a moment Jody thought he wasn't going to. His face looked dark, angry. But when he spoke, his voice was low and husky. "I see time passing. Chances and choices flying by. Things I can name, and things beyond. Eternity." He met her eyes, and his face softened. "And clouds . . . sometimes even a dragon or two."

"You're a nice person," she said softly.

He laughed. "You don't even know me. I might be a cad, an arch villian, a despicable character. I might be a liar. Or I might just be trying to seduce you."

"Or you might be trying to keep me at arm's length. Safe. Distant."

"I might."

"I can understand that. In today's world sometimes you have to. It can get too scary otherwise."

He frowned, his dark brows swooping low over clouded eyes.

Jody drew one finger tentatively across the furrows in his brow. "Of course," she added gently, "if you're too good at it, life can get too lonely to bear."

"No comment," he whispered. But he took her hand in his and laid it on his chest. "Besides, that's not what I want to talk about now. Look back up." He was giving orders again.

She did.

"Now think of yourself up there, floating on a cloud, looking down. What do you see?"

She drew a deep breath. *What do I see?* she mused. *Do I dare tell him? Do I take that chance?* She'd never been to Vegas, Reno, or Atlantic City. She played one dollar a week on the lottery, always the same six numbers. Had zero experience gambling. So she closed her eyes and went for the truth. "I see two people on a beach, on golden sand . . ."

"Yes?"

". . . surrounded by a million possibilities."

"What kind?"

She sighed, bet the bundle. "Lovely ones. Romance. Discovery. Happiness. It's the kind of place where *anything* can happen, remember?"

"And does it?"

Instead of answering, she rolled onto her side and said, "*Your* turn."

One dark brow rose slightly. "I'm not going to tell," he replied.

"What? No fair."

"Sorry. But it's my island. My rules."

"I'll remember that." She feigned a pout.

"Are you going to hold that against me?"

"I may, I may not; you'll have to wait and see."

"My pleasure."

She smiled, falling back onto the warm sand. "You know what? It is so easy to forget who you really are."

"That's why we're here," he whispered. "Because you have a strange way of seeing me that makes me feel at ease. As if you're seeing through me . . . into me. Making some strange connection between us."

Jody caught her breath, her playfulness forgotten. "You know something, Eric, I felt that from the minute you rescued me, before I even saw you, I *knew* who you were." She gave a soft, self-conscious laugh. "I felt, somehow, that

I knew *you.* In my dreams I felt it. It was your touch . . . your . . ." She fumbled for the right word, then gave up. "I don't know what to call it. And saying it out loud, it sounds a little crazy."

" 'A wee bit daft,' as my Scottish grandmother would say." He reached out and found her hand, lifted her palm to his lips, and kissed it, his breath warm on her sensitive skin.

She felt a rush of time, a whirl and swirl of years, her whole life so far racing to this moment. Could it be? Could it be that all those steps from little girl to woman had led her purposefully here, to this place, this moment? Was it possible?

There was a movement at her side, and she felt his breath on her lips, warm and sweet, so close, just the lightest of touches.

She opened her eyes, reached up, and touched his shaggy mane, brushing the hair back from his forehead.

He looked at her, deep into her eyes. "For all I know, you may have some terrible faults, Ms. Conners."

"So may you, Mr. Ransom. We'll just have to find out."

He smiled. Then he flopped down on his side, rested his head on her shoulder, and made himself comfortable. "Am I too heavy?" he asked.

Instead of answering, she unfolded one arm and placed it lightly around the muscular curve of his shoulder. Her fingers traced the sunlight on his warm skin. The feel of him made her tremble. *Amazing*, she thought. *Absolutely amazing.*

Moments later Eric and Jody heard the rumble of an engine, and watched as Chandler made the seaplane climb, dip its wing in salute, and disappear east into the sun.

"Well, there goes your ride back to civilization."

"That's okay," Jody said. "I'll take my chances right here."

"You might be sorry."

"Might be, but I doubt it. Anyway, if I wanted a guarantee, I'd buy a refrigerator."

He laughed, and she could feel it right through his chest, through her skin, deep in her bones. Again she trembled.

She was having trouble keeping it all in perspective, all sorted out. The fact that he was Eric Ransom made her feel as if she knew him; his face was familiar, his voice, even that sexy laugh. And yet he was a stranger, a man she'd just met, a man who turned her on, excited her in an unexpected, unfamiliar way.

Here he lay, his cheek on her shoulder, and she was trembling. Usually, she didn't like to be cuddled, didn't like social kisses, casual touching. There was so damn much of it, and none of it meant anything. But here he was, lying next to her, and just that alone had her trembling.

She might be sorry, he had said. Was he warning her? Teasing her? Laughing at her . . . or himself? She didn't know. But she wouldn't have left without taking this chance. There was always the possibility that magic did exist in the world, and that she would find a bit of it.

"What are you thinking?" he asked, touching her cheek.

"Nothing, just watching the clouds," she lied, blushing even as she said it.

Eric grinned, touched his fingers to her lips, and stroked them gently. Then he leaned over her and placed his mouth on hers, gently . . . in merely the shadow of a kiss, a cloud's breath.

Jody kissed him back, lifting her face to his, wanting more, her eyes shining. "This is better than the movies," she whispered.

Eric froze. Then he rolled away, leaving her shoulder cold and bare. Getting to his feet, he stared out at the water, hands stuffed into his pockets.

"This was a mistake," he growled.

With Chandler and the plane gone, he felt as if his safety net had been yanked away. There he was, on the high wire, alone, balancing his whole life in his hands, juggling it all . . . with nothing but empty space below. Didn't he ever learn? Damn.

Jody watched the play of emotions sweep across his face. She saw it all, but still couldn't believe her ears. "What, Eric?" she asked. "I must have heard you wrong."

"You heard me right: This is a mistake. You should have gotten on that plane."

Jody got up, brushing sand off her bottom and the backs of her legs. "What did I do? What's going on? One minute you're all warm and charming, and the next you're cold as ice. I don't get it."

"There's nothing to get," he said shortly.

"Which is fine, 'cause there's nothing I want," she snapped back, stung by his tone. "Or do you think you're so famous, so irresistible, that I'm going to throw myself at your feet and beg to go to bed with you?"

"It's happened before." He was facing her now, dark eyes smoldering.

"Oh. Well, that explains the clothes in the closet. But you know something? That has nothing to do with me. That's not *my* fault."

"Nobody said it's your fault. It's my own. I just don't learn—"

"Oh, poor you, all that fame and wealth and glamour—"

"You don't know anything about it!"

"No, I don't." She looked at him, put aside her hurt feelings and really *looked* at this man, and saw all the pain and bitterness etched on his handsome face. She would have taken her words back if she could. Instead, she went on more softly, "I didn't mean to sound like that, insensitive, defensive. You're right, I don't know anything about your life. But I assume that you chose it because it was what you wanted."

"I didn't *choose* it. You don't *choose* it. It's a passion, an addiction almost: Instead of the dope, the joint, the booze, it's the lights, the set, the role . . . the becoming someone else, and doing it so well, so completely, that everyone believes you. They see you up there on the screen, and they think it's you, they think they know you, love you or hate you, want you . . . and they don't know you at all. And sometimes you don't know yourself. Sometimes you lose it, you forget what's real and what's the role, and you carry it with you out into your life. Life . . .ha!" He gave a bitter laugh. "*That's* a joke! What life? People wanting, needing, taking little bits of you . . . this deal, that deal, everything's up for grabs, your time, your privacy . . . even your soul. You try to meet friends for a drink, or take your wife to dinner, eat at a restaurant, take a walk and there's somebody whose whole purpose in life is to catch you doing it. The camera in your face, the flash, the mike, the probing and prodding and goading."

He was sweating, beads of sweat standing across his upper lip. But his eyes were hard, remote, expressionless.

"So you got out," she whispered, watching his face.

He gave her a cold and cutting look. Narrowed his eyes. Tightened his mouth into a thin, hard line. "Yes. And I intend to stay out."

She nodded, holding his dark, unflinching gaze. "I can understand that, Eric," she said. "What I *don't* understand is why you're so afraid of *me*."

"What?" He laughed as if she'd made a joke and shook his head in disbelief. "What's that supposed to mean?"

"Just that I think that *this*"—she lifted both shoulders, searching for the right words—"this whole scene is just a role you're playing. It's not you. No, nobody could be that warm one minute, that cold the next, that trusting and then that bitter . . . that sensitive and then that cruel."

He looked down at her for a split second, hesitating. Then he said, "You're wrong," and started to turn away.

"I'm not," she challenged, chin up.

"No? Let me tell you: Practice makes perfect. Yes, I've brought women here before. Occasionally. Regrettably. Because it gets too lonely to bear . . . as you yourself were quick to point out. So you give in, you give in to the weakness, the hope, the wish . . . but it's always the same: Five minutes after we get here, I know it's never going to work. And sometimes . . . sometimes it's even lonelier than being by yourself."

"That was before. That wasn't *me*."

His smile showed a flash of teeth, all hard and glinting. "And you're different? What are you? A guardian angel? A fairy princess? Where's your magic wand, honey?" he mocked. "Where are my three wishes? My magic carpet—"

"Stop it!"

His head snapped back as if she'd struck him.

He glared at her, and Jody was sure he was going to say something else. But instead, he turned and strode off across the sand.

She watched him go, the sand flying up from his angry steps, the space between them widening in silence. In a moment he had disappeared around the corner of the house.

Jody stood there, watching the place he had been.

Disappointment crept over her, so sharp it hurt. Head down, she walked back along the beach alone.

Six

Jody bumped into Lena in the kitchen. There were mangoes and papayas piled all over the kitchen table, and pots simmering on the stove. The air was filled with a sweetness laced with spice, delicious, exotic; Jody could almost taste the aroma on her tongue. It brought her to a halt.

"My fruit preserves. Best in the world," Lena said modestly. "You'd like a taste?" Obviously, others had stopped to beg for a spoonful.

Jody let the luscious flavor fill her head and calm her spirit. She sank into a kitchen chair. "*This* is how I should have spent my morning. Everything else is too hard." She gave a forlorn sigh.

Lena looked at her. "What is too hard, girl?"

"Everything. Men. The whole thing."

"Men in general, or some specific man?"

"Both." She wound her legs around the chair legs and leaned her elbows on the table. "They're all the same."

"This one is different," Lena assured her.

"I don't think so. I mean, you like them, you open up, let them inside you, and the next thing you know, they either want everything, or they don't want anything at all. They want to own you, or they're headin' for the door."

"Uh-huh."

"You don't think so? I'm telling you, it's the truth nowadays. You live here on this island with Matthew, but the world out there is getting stranger every minute. It's scary. You meet a man, you think he's nice, and he turns out to be: A . . . married, B . . . a sex maniac, C . . . more interested in himself than you, or D . . . all of the above." She sighed. "What happened to romance?"

"It's still around. You just have to be: A . . . lucky, B . . . patient, C . . . willing to risk your heart, or D . . . all of the above."

"It still doesn't happen."

"Well, maybe you're right, girl. Like you said, here I am on this island. With Matthew. Content to be here. Maybe I don't know any longer what the real world is like."

Jody frowned, nibbling on an overripe slice of papaya. "Tell me . . . what's *he* like?"

"Ah, so we are going from generalities to the specific?"

"Yes. Tell me. Please?"

"It's not my place, girl. Not my right. Eric

would have to tell you himself. Besides, he's the only one who really knows."

"I don't think he does know. One minute he's one person, the next minute he's someone completely different."

Lena shook her head. "Oh, he knows all right. That man is something special."

"Is he?" Jody's voice was just a whisper. Her thoughts were swirling, bubbling and swirling like the sweet fruit in the pan on the stove. "He is, isn't he? I thought so. I don't mean because he's Eric Ransom, the movie star . . . no. It's something in his eyes, his face . . . something I can almost but not quite name. . . . Oh, but he turned so cold." She drew a breath, lifting her shoulders in bewilderment. "I don't know. And he may never *let* me know. He may send me home before I ever get to find out."

"The plane is gone." Lena smiled.

"But there's a boat. And the way he sounded, I think he'd give me a canoe and a paddle and wish me luck."

"Maybe."

Jody rested a hand on Lena's wrist. "Will he? Do you think he will? Or will he let me stay?"

Before she could answer, there were footsteps outside on the porch. The kitchen door swung open, and Eric walked in.

"Lena, I'm taking the boat out. Tell Matthew, please."

"He's not going with you?"

"No." He paused. "I'm going alone."

"Can I make you some sandwiches?"

"No thanks. I'm not hungry."

"You'll be back for dinner?"

"I'm not sure."

Jody watched it all like a spectator at a tennis match, head swiveling back and forth from one to the other. She kept waiting for one of them to glance at her, but neither did. Finally, she could stand it no longer and said, "Can I go?"

He looked at her in surprise. Wary. "I'm going alone."

"I won't be in the way. Besides, you said you'd show me where the herons nest. And maybe I can find some shells or something to take back to school to show the children."

"You can find those on the beach."

Jody crossed her arms over her chest. "Look, Eric, I'd like to go. May I?"

He hesitated, then shrugged. "Suit yourself. But I'm leaving now."

"I'm ready." She scrambled to her feet and followed him out the door.

"Can I help?" She was sitting in one of the big fishing chairs at the stern, out of the way, watching Eric as he untied the boat from the dock.

"Nope," he said, and swung lightly aboard. In a second he was standing behind the captain's chair, starting the engine, then easing the boat gently away and into the current. It was a beauty of a boat, about thirty-five, forty feet and outfitted for deep-sea fishing. The rods waved over her head like magic wands as the breeze whispered magic words.

She stepped up behind him. "Can I steer?"

"No." He gave her one of his dark, stubborn looks and then pretended to ignore her.

Deciding not to take offense, she went to the rail and leaned over. The wind pulled at her hair like a hand, yanking it back, whipping the ends around her cheeks. The air smelled of salt, a fishy, swampy smell that was strangely exciting; any moment she expected to see an alligator, only its eyes above water, the rest a dark, gliding underwater shape.

"There! A cormorant! Look!" she shouted. "And there on the log, there've got to be six . . . no, seven, eight! . . . turtles. Look at them all!

> *Over in the meadow,*
> *in the sand and the sun*
> *lived an old mother turtle*
> *and her little turtle one.*
> *'Snap!' said the mother,*
> *'I snap!' said her son,*
> *So they snapped and were glad*
> *in the sand and the sun."*

She chanted happily, her clear voice rising and falling with the singsong melody of the simple childhood rhyme.

"Remember that?" she asked Eric.

"No," he said, trying to keep an icy distance. It was hard work.

"Want to hear another chorus?" she asked, tipping her chin up and looking at him from under her lashes. " 'Down in the meadow . . . in the—"

"I'm *not* four years old."

"I'm appealing to the little boy inside you."

"There *is* no little boy inside me."

"Of course there is!" she chided, shaking her head. "There sure is a little girl inside me."

"Obviously," he said dryly.

"Ha-ha," she answered. "But that's better than keeping your inner self all locked up, hidden away."

"Thank you, Dr. Freud."

"You're welcome." She leaned back against the rail, feet apart to help keep her balance as the boat skimmed through the mangroves and out toward open water.

By noon they were out in open water. It was hard to tell in which direction they were heading, with the sun pinned straight up overhead, but Jody was not about to ask. She was just glad to be here.

Eric's aloofness had an unexpected perk. She was free to observe him, to watch his movements without fear of being caught at it. She studied his face, which was new to her eyes and yet known in that strange way that made her feel already connected to him. He squinted against the sun, lines creasing around his eyes, which were secretive. His dark hair whipped across his brow. He whistled constantly, just off-tune enough to make her want to do it for him once, the *right* way, but she bit her tongue. Whistling and scanning the horizon, he seemed totally oblivious to her.

So she took advantage of the situation. She let her eyes travel slowly down his body, across the broad shoulders, narrow hips, long legs. He was one fine-looking man, and it was a pleasure just to sit in the warm sun, the cool breeze, and look. She'd never spent a more contented morning!

Pushing with her bare feet, she made the big fishing chair swivel from side to side. She had been deep-sea fishing before, years ago, with her dad, when the two of them went out from North Miami on a big, smelly party boat. Shark, that's what her dad had caught: a hammerhead shark about six feet long, with small, ugly eyes on the far edges of his wide, flat head. That shark had hung on her dad's patio wall until he and her mom finally sold the place and moved to a condo. Now they kept parakeets, and a pair of rosy-cheeked lovebirds in a cage.

What would they think of this man?

His fame would make them shy, tongue-tied.

But they'd like his smile, his voice. Her mother would like his sensitivity, his words like poetry. Her dad would like his humor, and the easy way he handled this boat.

Jody watched his broad hands on the steering wheel, the tanned backs of his hands, the muscular, tanned forearms, the bunch and roll of muscle in his upper arms and shoulders as he steered. He was beautiful to watch. Skilled, confident, quiet, and sure in every movement.

He stood there, perfectly content just as he was, oblivious to her presence.

Seemingly.

Then he turned his head and looked at her over his shoulder. He could have been looking at a cloud, a bird, a flower, so quietly did he study her. It made her heart beat fast, dreadfully fast, but she didn't say a word, just returned his long, dark look.

And then, as if he'd satisfied himself about some question, he nodded once.

"How ya doin'?"

"Fine, thanks," she answered.

"You're not getting wet back there, are you?"

"No, not a drop. It's warm and wonderful."

"Getting hungry?"

"Not really." She shrugged. "I can eat if you want to."

"Well, if you don't mind doing the work, there's some cheese and crackers in the galley below, and some cold beer."

"Great. I'll be right back."

She went below, holding on to the railing as she took the steps slowly, carefully. Here she really felt the movement of the sea, the rise and fall of all that great moving power. It made her feel small, fragile . . . and claustrophobic. Hurriedly, she set cheese, crackers, napkins, and two beers on a tray and balanced them carefully as she climbed back up to the deck.

"Here you are," she said, setting the tray down on top of the sonar panel, and picked up one of the bottles of beer. "I forgot the opener."

"I'll get it for you," Eric said. He flipped the top off with the ball of his thumb.

"My hero," Jody teased, and took a long, cold drink.

"Feeling okay?" he asked, giving her a quick once-over.

"I was until I went downstairs."

"Below," he corrected.

"Below," she repeated, taking another long drink. "I don't like it down there. Nope . . . this sailor needs the wind in her face."

"Well, I can guarantee that for another couple of hours. Then we'll dock in Key West and pick up something to eat. Okay?"

"Of course." Tucking her feet up under her, she helped herself to cheese and crackers. Chewing thoughtfully, she waved a cracker at him. "Wait a minute. How can you go to Key West? Won't you be recognized?"

"I'll take care of that, don't worry."

"Me, I'm not worried about anything," she said, then polished off her beer.

"You do adjust well to changing circumstances, don't you?"

"One of the prerequisites for dealing with three-, four- and five-year-olds. It's either that or get ulcers. Besides, this isn't very hard to adjust to. I can handle this . . . with my eyes closed." She closed her eyes and tipped her face up to the sun. "Ummmm, this is wonderful."

"More wonderful than usual," Eric said softly.

Jody opened one eye and looked at him. "Wait a minute. Are we having another mood swing here? Another visit by Dr. Jekyll and Mr. Hyde?"

He took a long, relaxed swallow of beer. "I don't know what you're talking about."

"No, huh? Well then I won't bother to remind you of your strange behavior this morning."

"It wasn't strange," he insisted. "You just don't know."

"Know what?"

"What it's like . . . what it can be like. . . ." His voice drifted off, his eyes clouding. But Jody was not going to settle for that.

"More mysterious talk. Either tell me what you're thinking or don't, but don't hint at it and leave me dangling."

He looked at her, dark brows raised in surprise. "Bossy, aren't you?"

"No. Honest."

"Okay, then I'll be honest also. I'm attracted to you. I like you, though I'm not sure why." He shook his head. "But I don't know you. And I don't know if I can trust you."

"In what way?"

"With my life." He looked away from her, out to the horizon, but kept speaking, as though this was hard to say but needed saying. "Too many people need a role to play, a stage to play it on. They need special effects. They need an audience."

"Yes?"

He nodded slowly. His voice was harsh when he spoke again. "I've given too much of my life away to voyeurs, takers, holders-on. I was bled dry. I've got to hold on to the rest. I won't risk it."

"I told you, you have nothing to fear from me."

"That was when we were talking about my location, my . . . my whereabouts. Not my life. Not about caring . . . or touching."

"And does something I said or did this morning make you think I'd give you away? That I was playing a role? Or looking, as you put it, 'for a stage to play it on'?"

"No."

"And this morning? Was there an audience of thousands, and I just didn't notice?"

He looked at her. "I was afraid there was . . . in your imagination."

"Oh thanks, that's real complimentary," she drawled.

"I don't mean it to sound nasty. I just didn't know how *you* saw us. Whether any of the attraction was because you wondered what it would be like to have an audience, even one person you could tell about us. To . . . to . . . I don't know. . . ."

"To what? Go ahead and say it: to brag?"

"Maybe. Or just share it with, to heighten the excitement."

"Oh, that didn't need any heightening," Jody answered, feeling the blood rise across her throat, but keeping her eyes steady.

"Then you're a most unusual person."

"Of course," she said.

She made him laugh. He shook his head, grinning at her, his eyes warm and shining.

It made her brave—or foolish—again. "What would you have done if I hadn't insisted on coming along today?"

"I would have come alone."

"You wouldn't have asked?"

"No."

"You would have let me go home without getting to know me?"

"Yes. If you would have gone, then you weren't the right one anyway."

She swallowed. Waited a heartbeat. "What right one?"

He shrugged, as if he'd already said too much.

Jody was sure that if her heart wasn't stuck in her throat, she'd come right out and ask him again exactly what he meant. But she, too, felt suddenly reluctant to say more . . . to say anything out loud, out in the open. Instead, she got up out of the chair and walked over to him.

She stopped right in front of him and looked up into his eyes. Brown and bottomless, full of secrets and surprises. Sexy eyes. A Gypsy lover's eyes.

Reaching up, she put a hand against his cheek, feeling his skin and the contours of his bones.

He turned his face and kissed her palm, but kept his eyes on hers.

She put her other hand on his shoulder for balance, raised on tiptoe, and kissed him lightly on the corner of his mouth.

Slowly, he turned his face until his mouth found hers. He opened his lips and stroked her lips with his tongue, then pushed his tongue hungrily into her mouth. His arms wound tightly around her waist, and he pulled her up against his chest, hard, holding her tight against him, chest and hips. She could hardly breathe. The world was spinning.

The kiss was like a promise, an offering, a word spoken by lips that only touched, and needed to say nothing more. It was a moment of magic . . . and that was enough, wasn't it? Wasn't that more than most people could ask for in their whole lives: one moment of pure magic?

She stopped thinking and abandoned herself to the taste of him, the feel, the warmth and passion, as his lips alternated between bruising pressure and heart-stopping tenderness.

Oh, how the world spun. The sun was too bright, the sea too white, the whole world whirling, turning, tipping. She broke the kiss. "I think I'll sit for now," she said, feeling light-headed. "And later, when we're docked, we can talk."

"I don't want to *talk*." He grinned, wiggling his eyebrows at her in mock lasciviousness.

"Well, we'll talk about *that* too!"

When a dark smudge appeared on the horizon to the left, Eric slowed the boat to a crawl.

"Hold this for me, will you?" he asked, offering Jody the steering wheel. "I'll be right back."

"What do I do?" she asked.

"Aim straight ahead. Just keep the land to your left, the buoy to the right."

Jody squinted into the distance. "Oh, so that's land."

"Key West. And dinner. So hold her steady."

"Aye-aye, sir," she said, saluting smartly.

In three minutes, maybe less, Eric—or a man

she *assumed* was Eric—climbed back on deck from the cabin below. This man had a mustache, wraparound sunglasses, and a wide-brimmed straw hat.

"Nice," Jody commented. "Especially that hat. Nobody will give you a second glance."

"Not in Key West. I'm safe."

"What about me?" she asked. "Where's my disguise?"

"Why? Do you need one?"

"You bet. I could just be walking down the streets in Key West, and someone's liable to point at me and say, right out loud, 'Isn't that that preschool teacher from Orlando? I could swear it is! Quick, Myrtle, get the camera!'"

He grinned. "Tell me, does that happen often?"

"Only occasionally, but I think it's best to be prepared."

"Certainly," he drawled. "Okay, keep steering."

He vanished below and returned in a minute with another pair of sunglasses and a plaid golfer's cap.

"What? No mustache?" she teased.

" 'Fraid not." He placed the cap on her head, and she leaned toward him when he settled the sunglasses on her face.

She looked at him.

He looked at her.

"You'd better go sit down for a while and let me bring the boat in," Eric said huskily.

"Why?" she whispered.

"Because . . . if you don't . . . there's no telling what will happen. I'm only human."

Jody's first instinct was to make some kind of smart-aleck remark and see exactly what *would* happen. But Eric wasn't kidding. And her *heart* wasn't kidding; it was listening to her body, which was suddenly and completely awash with desire. But was she ready for this?

"I think I'll go sit down," she said, her breath warm against his lips.

"I think that's a good idea," he whispered back. But he caught her close and kissed her before he let her go. Then, with one hand, he took off his sunglasses and hat, *her* sunglasses and hat, and tossed them on the deck. He kissed her again. Hungry, hungry, their lips nipped and tasted each other, their mouths lifting and turning, fitting to each other only to part and fit again. He groaned, breathing hard.

"You too!" She was trembling, wet and trembling and melting all at the same time.

"Go sit down," he breathed.

"I'm trying to—"

"Go ahead."

"I will, I will. Just a minute, one minute more . . ."

"Okay. Okay okay okay . . . that's enough. . . ."

"I know . . . I know. . . ."

"Go. Go sit down. . . ."

"I'm trying."

Her breasts were aching, pressed hard against his chest. Her hands were buried in his thick dark hair. She held him, touched him, and kept kissing him.

He cupped her head between his hands and drank the kisses from her mouth. "Go . . . sit . . . down . . . Jody. Please . . ."

"I'm trying. . . . I'm trying. . . ."

"Go . . . go now. . . ."

"Yes . . . yes . . ."

His mouth left her mouth and traveled down her throat, brushing hot, wet kisses over her skin. Oh, how that silly mustache tickled as he moved his mouth down, down to the rise of her breasts. He lingered there, dusting her with hot, wet, hungry kisses. He opened the top button of her jumpsuit and nuzzled her skin, rubbing his cheek back and forth, kissing her gently at each pass, till she was faint with the feel of rough cheek, plundering mouth. Her eyes were closed, her head fallen back. She no longer thought, or heard or spoke; she only felt. . . . felt *him*, with every inch of her being.

"Jody? . . ." he whispered, lips against her skin.

"Yes? . . ."

"Jody. Are you saying 'yes'?"

"What? . . ." she breathed, tipping her head down, burying her face in his dark tangled hair. "Hmmmm? What?"

"Jody, I'm asking you: What are you saying?"

Whether it was the rough, gravelly edge to his voice or the words themselves, she didn't know, but suddenly she did know *exactly* what he was asking, and that the decision was hers. She squeezed her eyes shut, wishing for the sweet, mindless oblivion of passion. She knew this was a moment of magic . . . *knew* it was a fairy tale come true . . . and *knew* it couldn't last. Oh, *that* thought was like a knife in her heart!

Pushing her fingers through his hair, she looked deep into his eyes. Then she shook her head ever so slightly and, breathing through parted lips, she whispered, "I guess I'd better go sit down."

"Then go sit *down*," he groaned.

But he nipped at her skin before he stepped away, and held her hand for another half minute before he really let her go. "It's all right now. I'll dock the boat, and we'll get us some dinner. Okay?" There was a barely perceptible hint of sadness in his voice, a faint echo of her own confused emotions.

She nodded, not ready to trust her voice. Afraid if she opened her mouth, she'd cry, *I don't care about reality. I don't care about tomorrow. I want happiness today. I want you, Eric. Hold me. Love me!*

The feeling was so strong, she dared not even look at him. She sat at the stern and watched the land draw near.

Seven

It had to have been 100 degrees in Key West that afternoon. The gorgeous breeze that had accompanied the boat all day decided to wait offshore for their return; there wasn't a trace of it in town. Instead, the air was filled with that sense of a party happening just around the corner that was so uniquely Key West. The streets were crowded, and the sidewalk cafés were jammed with natives and tourists vying noisily for an inch of space and a cold drink. Every few minutes either the Conch Train or a tour bus rattled by, loudspeakers blaring. Jimmy Buffett mixed with reggae, jazz, and blues, spilling from dim bars and shaded terraces.

Eric avoided the tourist traps. Holding her hand, he led Jody deep into the old neighborhoods with their shaded, winding streets where gingerbread-trimmed houses perched on hurricane-wary raised foundations. Flowers spilled out of back porches in wild abundance. Birds chirped and screeched and sang from moss-draped live oaks and rustling palms.

"Where are we going?" Jody asked.

"To a little market I know. I thought we'd buy a couple of lobsters and some fresh fruit and champagne . . . if that sounds all right to you."

"It sounds wonderful," she agreed. "Is it much farther?"

Eric slowed and looked at her, head to toe. "We have got to get you some clothes of your own, Jody."

"Oh, don't you think this suits me?" She plucked at the baggy, rolled-up jumpsuit.

"Definitely a bad fit." He gave a quick shudder of memory and grabbed her hand again. "Come on, we'll take care of that. Immediately!"

On a side street was a small boutique, its window offering Armani, Adrienne Vittadini, Ralph Lauren.

"Oh, too rich for my blood . . ." Jody frowned, pulling back from the door. She felt uncomfortable already.

"Sorry, but it'll have to do. It's here, we're here, and the lobsters are around the corner. Trust me," he said, and held the door open for her.

The proprietor was a dark-skinned beauty, hair cut short and severe to accentuate her lovely face, with perfect legs and a flawless figure. Jody was quickly intimidated. But the woman, faced with a strange man in a straw hat and fake mustache and a woman in borrowed clothes, was as nice as could be.

In less than ten minutes Jody was dressed in shorts and a top, both of which fit perfectly, a new pair of sandals, and the laciest, sexiest underwear she'd ever owned.

When Eric glanced quizzically at the last two figures on the bill, Jody blushed beet red. But he didn't say anything. Not a word. Simply counted out the cash, told the owner to toss the jumpsuit, and took Jody's hand again.

Jody must have looked different, as marvelous as she felt, because people passing on the street turned and stared. They smiled. They nodded hello.

Jody smiled and nodded back. She hummed. She swung the hand that held Eric's hand, feeling like a kid again, free and happy, hopeful, sure of the joy and goodness of life. And that part of it was meant for her.

This part: this day, this man, this feeling.

Eric saw the smile tipping her lips and felt a strange and unexpected pull at his heart.

Watch it, he thought, *watch your step.* But it was impossible with this woman at his side. And besides, it felt so good to let down the walls, to relax, not to be on guard. It felt damn good. It chased the dark thoughts out of his brain and made him want to—

"Jody?" came the shriek, almost in his ear. "Jody Conners, is that you?"

A woman was barreling toward them, husband in tow.

Jody blanched. Her hand stiffened in his. Eric released her, stepping back even as Jody stuttered in surprise, "Oh, oh . . . Mrs. Forde, Dr. Forde. Hi. How nice to see you both."

"Why, Jody Conners, it *is* you! I said it was you, though I never expected to see you down here. I guess I never expect to see you *anywhere* but the Hundred Acre Woods. Oh, we moms do love that place. And you too, Jody! Thomas had such a wonderful year; you know, I do believe that a child's third year is absolutely critical . . . don't you agree, dear?"

She jerked her husband's attention back to the conversation, but her eyes, following his, caught sight of Eric's disappearing back. "My goodness, we didn't interrupt anything, did we? I certainly didn't mean to chase your friend away. You won't believe this"— she leaned close, her voice a loud stage whisper—"but that man you were with looked *so* familiar. . . ."

Lifting one brow, she awaited Jody's reply.

Jody was dumbstruck. She felt as though she'd been run over by a truck, then asked to explain the wreck. "Oh . . . oh, well." She laughed nervously. "That was . . . Herman. He just went to buy some . . . uh, some bologna for dinner. He'll be back. No problem." She smiled. Shrugged. Looked from one parent to the other. "Well, say hi to Thomas for me."

"We will." Mrs. Forde put her hand on Jody's arm, detaining her. "Jody, you won't believe who that man reminded me of. From way over there, across the road, I said, 'Philip, doesn't that man look familiar? Like that famous movie star who disappeared a few years back? And isn't that *our* Jody with him?' " Again, those piercing eyes, waiting, watching.

"Ah . . . ha-ha! What a funny thing!" Jody laughed. "Usually, people say he looks like . . . uh, that baseball player. You know who I mean." She snapped her fingers. "Ummm, what *is* his name? Anyway, gotta go . . . or the tour bus'll leave without me. 'Bye!"

And she dashed off.

As she rounded a corner, a hand pulled her into a doorway. It was Eric, hat pulled way down over his face, scowling. "Sorry I took off like that," he muttered.

"It's okay." She dropped back into the shadows next to him, hugging her arms around herself. "That's not fun, is it?" she said. "You must hate it. You want to say, 'Hey, yes, it's me. But just leave me alone. Give me a little space here.' "

"You didn't say that, did you?" he asked quickly.

"No," she answered. "I don't believe this happened."

"Neither do I. I've come to Key West before. No one ever stopped me, bothered me . . . noticed me." He rubbed at the muscles in the back of his neck. "Damn, that was close!" But a smile was now glinting in the shadows in his eyes. He took her hand. "I didn't know you were such a dangerous woman to be with."

"Wait," she said. "You haven't seen anything yet."

"No?" he asked, caution slipping from him like a cloak. It left him unmasked: bold, sexy . . . unmistakably Eric Ransom.

If anyone caught a glimpse of him now, there'd be no doubt who he really was, Jody thought. Out loud she said only, "Let's get those lobsters and head for the boat," batting her eyelashes at him in mock seduction. But she looked both ways before she stepped from the shadows of the doorway.

"Lobsters. Champagne. What can you do to top that, Mr. Ransom?"

"Are you open to all suggestions?" he asked, grinning at her over the rim of his glass.

It was a wicked grin—loose, hot—and it suited Jody just fine.

Here on the boat she felt released, removed from the ordinary world. It was like stepping back into the realm of fairy tales and magic: Champagne could flow like water . . . could be sipped from glass slippers . . . *anything* was possible.

And everything was perfect. Beneath her, the boat rocked at anchor in a quiet cove about a mile from Key West. Around her, the ocean was turquoise and gold, the wavelets tipped pink by the setting sun. Above her, the sky was a dark blue canopy reaching to heaven. And inside her . . . well, inside her was a hot, bubbling excitement that licked along her nerves and set her skin tingling.

She felt the way she imagined a sky diver must, perched at the door of the plane, about to leap out into the wildly desired unknown.

"Mm-hmm," she said, returning his grin. "Just give me a hint of what you have in mind."

Putting down his glass, he leaned over and kissed her lightly on the mouth, his tongue just tasting the sweetness of her lips. "Will that do for a hint?"

She ducked her head and laughed. "Listen to us. We sound like a grade-B movie."

"No! Don't say that, Jody." He shook his dark head, frowning down at her. "No movies. I want you to feel the real me, *know* the real me."

Suddenly, Jody could hardly speak. She took his face in her hands. "Oh, Eric, you mean that, don't you? You do. I never thought I'd find a man who'd say that. I only *dreamed* I would."

"This is no dream." He leaned down until his breath was warm on her mouth. Her eyes fluttered and closed. Her lips parted. And then he kissed her passionately, stealing her breath, her soul . . . her very being.

She gave herself up to the taste of him, the sweetness of his mouth, the rough brush of his hair beneath her hands, the hard press of his chest against her breasts . . . his warmth, his smell, his feel . . . his skin, his muscles, his solid strength. There was power in his touch, fierceness in his kiss, hunger in his embrace.

Clearing a space on the deck with a quick sweep of his arm, he laid her down and then lay on top of her. She took the feel of his weight in every pore, every inch of skin, savoring it, loving it. She groaned in pleasure, not meaning to. She couldn't help herself. This was all that she'd been longing for, aching for, waiting for, all her life. This was the man, the moment . . . no matter what waited ahead.

Again a little growl of desire rose in her throat. She buried her face against his neck, nuzzling at his warm skin, licking his skin with her tongue. He tasted wonderful, delicious . . . she could just eat him up.

Eric seemed to have the same idea. Hungrily, he was kissing her eyes, her cheeks, her lips, nose, chin, and on down her throat and across her breasts. Lifting himself up over her, he bent his head way down and tongued her nipples through the soft knit of her shirt.

She fell back, hands wide, shivering with pleasure. And then, without knowing it, she was arching her back, lifting her breasts to his mouth, clutching his thick, rough hair in her hands and urging his mouth on and on.

She writhed in pleasure, wanting more, wanting the feel of his wet mouth on her nipples, wanting the rub of his skin against her skin, his hair, his heat, his hardness there, pressed against her—all-taking, all-yielding, and all-giving, satisfied for once, finally.

Now. Now. She groaned aloud, deep in her throat, the sound rising from her heart, her flesh, her quickened blood and throbbing pulse. Now. *Now.*

"Come," he whispered, lifting his weight off her for a moment. He rocked back on his heels and slipped an arm under her shoulders, one behind her knees. "Come. We'll go below, down to the cabin. Now." He was as breathless as she, as trembling, as hungry. "I'll carry you. . . ."

"No . . . no, I don't want to go below. Do we have to?"

"No, we don't. Right here is fine. Right here . . . right now." Grabbing the bottom of his shirt, he yanked it over his head and tossed it across the deck. He kicked off his sandals. He reached down to unbutton his pants.

Jody said softly, "Let me. Please?"

Eric closed his eyes and let his hands fall to his sides. "My pleasure," he breathed.

Her hands were shaking, but slowly, surely, she undid the button, slid down the zipper. She pulled the opening wider, revealing the taut tan skin of his stomach, the top edge of his briefs, a few dark hairs curling out from under the white elastic band, and the bulging white cotton.

Like a teenager, she drew a sharp, quavering breath, that gasp that meant discovery and arousal. She wanted to touch him. She was afraid to touch him. She was afraid to even look, afraid—

"I'm dying here, girl," he murmured, letting his head fall back between his shoulders. "You're killing me."

So she touched him, lightly, lovingly, then pressed her palm against the heat and power of him.

He shuddered.

She drew his pants down over his hips until she could see the hard angles of his hipbones, the darkly tanned skin of his thighs.

Her eyelids fluttered. Her fingertips trembled. She wasn't even breathing. Pants first. Then briefs. Then there he was: naked, beautiful.

"Jody . . ." he said softly, her name a sound that was almost pain.

She drew her fingernails up and down his back, tracing the bunched outlines of his muscles, running her palms over his ribs. She slid her hands down to the small of his back, the base of his spine, then fanned them out over the hard curve of his buttocks.

He dropped down on top of her, breathing hard into her hair, holding her so close, she was almost part of his body: knees, thighs, groin, hips, stomach, chest . . . one. She felt his pulse in her bones, heard it in her head and heart.

He kissed her mouth. "I have to have you. Have to know every inch of you, every sound, every smell, every taste."

"Yes," she whispered. "I want you too."

"Now?"

"Yes, now." She spoke around her kisses, her mouth brushing his lips, his eyes, his chin.

He hefted his weight off and rolled onto his side, his hands cupping her face. "You're sure?"

"Absolutely sure," she answered.

"Then I'll be right back," he said, heading below.

"Eric—"

"One minute . . . just one minute, I promise."

Jody had time only to unstrap her sandals and pull some cushions down onto the deck. She laid her head back on one as he returned and knelt beside her, holding a small foil packet.

"If that's what I think it is, I'm a very happy woman," she whispered as her eyes traveled over the beauty of his body. "And if I ruled the world . . . you'd never wear clothes again."

"It gets chilly here at night."

"Oh, I'd keep you warm!"

"Then you really want to make love with me?"

"Yes. Truly."

The look he gave her seemed to bare his soul. His voice was rough with unused emotion. "I've been alone for a long time."

"So have I. On an island of *my* own. Right there in the middle of Orlando, surrounded every day by other people's children, some friends and relatives. Still . . . in the world today it feels like we're all separate. Alone."

"But there have been other men?"

"Once. But restraint hasn't been hard. Everyone says I want too much, but I wasn't going to settle for less. All around me people settled for less, and they weren't happy. Not really *happy*. No . . . I've been waiting, dreaming, for a long time. Ever since I was a teenager and believed everything was going to be lovely and easy. It isn't, is it?"

"No," he answered gently, "it isn't."

"No. But now . . . this . . ." She touched his chest with her fingertips. " . . . *you*. All this was worth the wait, the loneliness."

"But, Jody, what does that mean? Have you thought about the future? About us? About what—"

"Shhhh," she said, covering his lips with hers. "That's all part of later. *Now* there's just you and me. Us together. Here"— she kissed his chin—" . . . and *here* . . ."—she kissed his throat—" . . . and *here* . . ."—she kissed his chest—" . . . and here . . ." She drew her lips over his ribs till her mouth rested above his heart, and she could feel its furious drumming.

Quickly, she sat up and pulled her top over her head. For a minute she was stuck, the buttons at the neck catching in her salt-tangled hair.

Eric took quick advantage of her disadvantage. He pressed his face against her honey-colored skin, the fullness of her breasts just barely hidden by creamy lace. "Nice bra," he whispered, his warm mouth against first one hidden nipple, then the other.

"Thank you. I hoped you'd like it," she breathed.

"Are there panties to match?"

She nodded, trembling, her hands shaking as she fumbled with the top button of her shorts.

"Wait," he said softly. "Let me do that."

Jody caught her breath. Her throat was dry with something close to fear, but everywhere else she was all at once wet, so wet.

Eric curved his body up to hers, shifting so that she kneeled between his legs.

Light-headed, Jody rested her hands on his thighs to keep her balance. His skin was warm, firm, the short curly hairs just a tickle beneath her palms.

But as he kissed her, every feeling became magnified, separate and distinct and overwhelming. The press of his mouth to hers, the smoothness of his lips, the hardness of his teeth, the raspy surface of his tongue as it searched her mouth. The faint scent of butter and wine on his breath. The salty smell of his hair. The heat rising off his body, carrying its own musky, erotic scent. The tension tightening the muscles in his thighs, and the brush of fuzzy hair beneath the unbearably sensitive skin of her palms.

Each feeling traveled along the pathways of her nerves to her brain, to her heart, to the innermost core of her being. Excitement rose like heat. Her blood was a drum, beating, throbbing within her. Lights danced behind her closed eyelids, keeping time to her ecstatic pulse.

When she felt his hands at her waist, she stopped breathing. When he tugged the shorts down over her hips, she thought she'd faint. Then he reached down and touched her. She was so ripe, so full, like a bud unfolding, opening . . . and his hand was the warm touch of the sun.

She moaned in pleasure.

Pulling her down on top of him, Eric clasped her to his chest, wrapping his legs around her legs. His voice was a prayer, a song in her ear. "Heaven help us, Jody. I think I really love you."

Taking his face between her hands, she kissed him long and hungrily. "I love you too. And I want to make endless, delicious love with you, Eric Ransom."

He believed her. He *had* to. She didn't— couldn't—know the depth of the loneliness he'd suffered, the despair. To have her in his arms, to hold her, touch her, love her . . . it was more than he could refuse. It would have taken the strength of Apollo, the sleep of Morpheus, the wine of Dionysus, to relinquish her now.

And he was just a man.

And this might be just for a moment, but for a moment he'd have it. He'd take happiness now while he could. He *had* to. He'd hold her, touch her, make love to her, now.

He entered her.

Their bodies joined, became one. Wrapped in each other's arms, tangled in each other's legs, they moved together like entwined strands of seaweed urged this way and that by the ocean's tug. Adrift in their passion, they clung to each other, riding the rising waves of ecstasy. And as the crest of that wave broke and spilled within them, he called her name, and she answered.

Eight

The night air felt cool on her bare skin, so Jody used Eric as her blanket. She pulled his warm, muscular leg up across her thighs. Obligingly, his whole body followed.

"Not too heavy, am I?" he asked.

"Just right," she assured him. Snuggling down, she sighed happily.

The stars twinkled beyond the curve of his shoulder. Millions of light-years away, perhaps vanished already even as their glow reached her eyes, they seemed eternal, joyous, glorious. They filled the velvet sweep of sky, winking at her happily. She winked back. Never before had she felt so one with the universe. Never so safe. Never so happy.

"I love you," she whispered.

"I love you too."

She nuzzled her face into the warmth of his

skin. "You're not cold, are you . . . on top?" She rubbed her hands across the delicious skin of his bare back and buttocks.

"Not when you do that," he answered.

"Good. Then I can keep doing it?"

"Oh, . . . yes."

She laughed softly and kissed his neck.

The boat rocked on a dark, endless sea. The stars shone in the dark, endless sky. Jody and Eric floated somewhere in between, suspended in time and space.

"Talk to me," she said. "Tell me about your life, about Hollywood, the movies."

"Must I?" he asked, reluctance heavy in his voice.

"Please? I do want to know all about you, everything."

He gave a soft grunt of laughter. "The crash course? Ransom 101?"

"Yup, that's the one."

He took a deep breath. "Well, my family's from Scotland, via Montreal and then down into Wisconsin. My father built boats on Lake Michigan. I grew up there, in a little town called Manitowoc." He paused, smiling down at her. "It was great. I loved it, knew everyone, every inch of the town, the land, the boatyards."

"But you left?"

"It's tough to be an actor in Manitowoc, Wisconsin."

She traced the smooth fan of muscle across his back with her fingertips. "So you always wanted to be an actor?"

"It was suggested to me by my high school counselor. She thought it was a good alternative to juvenile delinquency, given my reputation for acting up in class."

"Ah. So you were a bad boy."

"*She* was nice enough to use the words 'spirited' and 'imaginative', dear one."

Jody giggled. "Lemme tell ya, from someone who's held plenty of parent-teacher conferences, the words 'spirited' and 'imaginative' always mean the kid who ate the crayons or poured the bucket of sand on the other kid's head. *'Spirited.' 'Imaginative.'* Ha! So they sent you to California."

"Actually, I was heading to New York. I was going to take acting classes and make it on Broadway. But the first ride I hitched turned out to be with a couple of college girls driving across country for the summer. One thing led to another, and they convinced me to head for Hollywood instead and become 'a movie star.'" He uttered the last three words with plenty of drama.

"Flattered you, huh, Ransom?"

"Yup. Sure did."

"So they turned around and took you to Hollywood?"

"Door to door. I took a screen test and got offered the part of the hometown hero in *After the War* . . . and that was that."

"That was that," she echoed. "Amazing."

"Sure as hell amazed me," he said with that same note of self-mockery. "Happened so fast, I didn't even see it coming. All of a sudden there were agents, offers, deals being made, and an entourage: people needing, fawning, coercing, always after a piece of the action. People calling at all hours of the day and night, and people waiting on my front lawn to see how I walked the dog, and requests for autographs, and pictures and a handshake, a kiss, a touch . . . a piece of clothing. I once had a woman beg me for one of my socks! God knows what she wanted to do with *that*." He snorted in disgust. "Too much. It was too much."

"But there must have been some fun: opening nights, and glamour and wealth. . . . It's what we all dream about when we see someone like you up on the screen."

"But you don't really see *me*. It's just an image, a role an actor plays. The *man* is different, seperate. And that man had his own hopes and fears, his own day-to-day life that he was trying to live, to find meaning in."

Jody could feel him tighten within himself and withdraw.

"Was it that bad?"

"Yes," he answered softly. "For me it was. Maybe I was too young. Maybe it had all come too easy. Maybe I was just naive. But I kept trying to make sense of it all, to find someone to ground me . . . an anchor, a refuge. . . ."

"Some port in the storm?" Jody mused.

"Yes."

"Did you find it? Did you find anyone?"

"I thought so. I met Françoise Deurat. We were filming *And Ever After*."

"I saw that. It was wonderful!"

"Thanks," he said, shaking his head. "Funny how different what the audience sees is from the reality of it all. Light years apart." He frowned, his eyes darker than the night sky.

"Oh. Was it terrible too?"

"Savage." He shook his head, then rolled off onto one elbow and looked away, out to sea, his face turned from her. "When we were first married, I thought it would work. I'd make it work. I hired a bodyguard. Bought a place in Oregon where we could hide out. But that was not at all what she had in mind. Her career was just starting, and the best thing that could happen to her was publicity. So we got plenty of it. No matter where we went, what we did, there was someone there, taking pictures, making snide remarks, trying to provoke some response. If I got angry at one too many flashbulbs in my face, one too many microphones, the articles that got written went for blood: *I* was nasty, ungrateful, an egomaniac, cold-blooded and hard-hearted—"

"You aren't!" Jody took his shoulders in her hands and pulled him down on top of her. She wrapped him in her arms. "You're a gentle, loving man."

"Think so?" he whispered into her hair.

"I know so. What about Françoise?"

A muscle jumped along the hard line of his jaw. "It was good for her career."

"Oh."

"There was a miserable divorce. Endless, disgusting."

"I remember."

"Of course. We were media fodder for months." He shook his head, brows bunched in pain. "Anyway, I finished the picture I was working on—"

"*Outcast?*"

"Yes, *Outcast.*"

"That is my favorite movie ever. You were so good, Eric, so wonderful. I'm just sorry it cost you so much."

He leaned his head against her shoulder and closed his eyes. "Thanks."

She stroked his hair. "You're welcome. And then? That was it?"

"That was it."

"You just vanished? Came here?"

"Vanished, yes. But first I tried Wisconsin. Grew a beard, rented an old cabin in the woods."

"But?"

"Went in to town for groceries one morning and found NBC waiting."

"Oh."

"So I shaved the beard, grew a mustache, and tried Costa Rica. A friend had a condo there."

"And?"

"The *National Enquirer.* You know how it is: Inquiring minds want to know."

Jody pressed her face against his chest and rubbed his back. "So, *then* here?"

"Yes. Here. Safe and unfound . . . until you."

"You're safe with me." Putting both hands against his chest, she pushed him up off her until she could see his eyes. "You *are* safe with me, Eric."

He smiled, used his weight against her small hands, and lay back on top of her. He kissed her mouth. "Okay. I trust you."

She answered him with a kiss to seal the words. "Ummmm . . . you kiss good, Mr. Ransom—at least all those steamy love scenes didn't go to waste."

"Thanks."

"Hey, I just thought of something. What about Chandler?"

"He works for me."

For a second she looked puzzled. "Funny, but something that was said made me think he was an actor—"

"He is. And he keeps an eye for me on the theater schools in Miami and New York."

"What theater schools?"

"The Workshop."

"The Workshop South? In Miami, down near Coconut Grove? I've heard of that. Aren't they even starting to do some traveling children's theater?"

"Yes."

"And there's another? In New York?"

"Yes."

"And *you* own them?"

"Yes. Through a dummy organization."

She narrowed her eyes, studying his face. "From what I heard, most of the students in Miami are there on scholarships. Lots of minority students. Lots of kids who couldn't pay for Yale Drama."

"Yes."

"I'm impressed." She tipped her head, nibbled on her lip. "But considering how you feel about acting—"

"I love acting," he said. "I love it and always will. I just couldn't survive Hollywood. But that doesn't mean it can't work for someone else. And maybe some of these kids'll end up on Broadway: the next James Earl Jones, the next Swoosie Kurtz. You never know."

She shook her head, looking deep into his eyes. "Nope, you never know."

"Or they could be directors, stage managers. They could be in lighting, or set design, or sound—"

"I get it, I get it," she broke in, laughing.

"Good. Then can I stop talking and get on to more important things?"

"There's nothing more important than two people getting to know each other," Jody declared with a mischievous grin. "Don't you agree?"

"Oh, I'm all for getting to know each other. I'd just like to stop *talking*."

He dropped his weight down on her, making her breath come out in a *whoosh* of surprise. He kissed her mouth before she could protest, kissed her chin and cheeks and nose, brushed his lips across her eyelids. "Are you panting because I'm wonderful, or because you can't breathe, darling?" he asked in her ear.

"Both!" she gasped.

He chuckled and, shifting his weight to one hip, he rolled over and lifted her up on top of him. She fit there neatly, the top of her head under his chin, her toes reaching to his ankles. Nice. Just right.

"Oh, I love the way you feel, Eric."

He wrapped his arms around her ribs, squeezing her tight. "Go ahead—talk dirty to me," he teased.

"Okay." She rested her chin on his chest. "I like the way you feel under me, the way your chest seems made for me to press my breasts against. I like the way your belly feels so hard and tight, curved in just perfectly so that my belly fits just right against it. I like the way my hips fit just between your hips. The way we fit together so perfectly for sex. The way—"

He groaned. "Stop right there, or I'm not going to be able to control myself much longer."

"My, my . . . but you are open to the power of suggestion, aren't you?"

"Not usually. Maybe you're a witch, and it's some magic power you're using on me. Enchanting me, stealing my soul."

"As you've stolen mine," she whispered.

"Oh, Jody." He breathed a sigh of longing, all teasing washed away in an instant. "Jody, you make me feel as though this is possible."

"It is."

"Jody—" he warned, shaking his head.

"It is, Eric." She cut him off, her hand pressed over his mouth. "It is. You and me. Here. Now. And these are my hands touching you. . . . Do you feel them? This is my mouth kissing you. . . . this kiss, and another . . . And these are my breasts, my skin, my tongue . . . all real. All now. All possible."

"All real . . . all possible . . ." he echoed, his eyes closing as he pulled her close. "Oh, Jody . . . you delight and excite me."

"Do I? Good!"

She kissed his face, then pushed herself up and away from him, hands balanced on his chest. Bending just her head, she kissed his throat, his shoulders. She kissed his nipples, making him groan and clench his fists. She kissed his ribs, tenderly, going down one side and up the other.

"Jody, Jody . . ." he whispered, twisting his head back and forth restlessly, eyes closed, lips parted. She watched him for a minute, savoring the delicious sense of power it gave her to see him caught in this passion of her making.

"Talk to me, Eric. Tell me . . ."

"Wait. Wait . . ." he panted.

"What? You want me to stop?" she asked innocently, moving her mouth down to his belly button, rubbing her face back and forth, letting her hair brush across his hot skin. "Should I stop, darling?"

"No, no. No, don't stop," he breathed, taking her shoulders in his hands. "No. Come here . . . come here. . . ."

But she resisted, kissing him into torment, her tongue and lips hungry for the warm, sweet taste of him. "What, Eric?" she teased, teasing herself into frenzy. "What now?"

"Come down here and I'll tell you."

"Why don't you just *show* me," she dared, her own voice an unfamiliar growl.

With amazing strength he lifted his body up to hers, catching her in his arms, finding her mouth with his and kissing her until her lips felt bruised and tender. She wrapped his head in her arms, relishing the roughness of his dark wild hair. His mouth found her breasts; his teeth closed gently on her nipples. Jody threw back her head, tears burning her eyes, a soft moan rising in her throat. "Oh yes, Eric, yes," she cried.

A moment's pause, a breath of night air on their heated skin, and then they were back together, locked in each other's arms.

When she came, she cried out. And a second later his own harsh cry broke from his throat. The two sounds flew up into the dark, endless sky, becoming one in the surrounding stillness.

It was only later that Jody heard again the soft lap of wave on hull, the occasional drift of laughter from the far shore. Against her cheek was the soft murmur of Eric's breath. But inside she was quiet, perfectly still and at anchor. Reaching up, she rearranged the cushion under her head, pulled Eric's shirt across her shoulders, snuggled into his warmth, and slept.

Nine

"Wake up, Jody. We've got to go."

"Hmm?" She made a little sleepy noise of protest. It took her a minute to get comfortable again on the wooden deck, and she was just sliding back into a dream when Eric's voice came again.

"Jody, wake up. Go below if you want to sleep. Here, let me help you." She felt his hand go under her shoulders.

"Ummmm," she purred, draping both arms around his neck. "Come back here. Come on, Eric, come back and keep me warm."

"Later," he said softly. "Right now, we're being watched."

Jody's eyes snapped open; suddenly she was wide awake. Realizing a light cotton blanket had been tossed over her, she gave a sigh of relief. "Thanks. Quick thinking, Mr. Ransom."

"Practice makes perfect," he said, an edge to his voice.

Shading her face with one hand, she looked up at him, and groaned. The fake mustache was back.

He glowered at something she couldn't see off to the right side of the boat. "Some sightseer or Peeping Tom's over there with binoculars. He was giving us a real once-over when I woke up."

Getting up on one elbow, she peeked between the deck and the rail. Not sixty feet away, another boat was anchored, and at the moment the man on the flying bridge was carefully focusing on the distant shore, pretending to search for birds, or coconuts, or some such thing. But who knew what he had seen? Or why he'd been looking?

Damn him anyway, for spoiling her morning and putting Eric in such a black mood.

She wrapped the blanket tightly around her. "How dare he?" she stormed. "I can see why it makes you furious. Being hounded, watched . . . oh, I want to go tell him to take a flying leap!"

She started to get to her feet, but Eric held her down. "It doesn't do any good, Jody. It's just what they want: to get a rise out of you, to prove they can. It's better just to ignore him—"

"And let him think he can get away with it? I will not!"

"And when he starts taking pictures, calls the newspapers, feeds 'em a hot story? Who's won then?"

"Well, we certainly haven't won by going below to hide."

"I *wasn't* going below," Eric snapped. "I was sending *you* below to keep you safe."

She could see she'd hurt him . . . again. Damn! "I'm sorry. I didn't mean to get mad at you. Go ahead and do what you think is best; I'll go down and get dressed." Bunching the blanket to her chest, she hurried to the stairs leading below. "Back in a minute."

"Take your time. I'm gonna get us out of here."

"Where do you want to go?" she asked softly.

"Far away from here," he swore through clenched teeth. "Scotland, maybe. Go off to Scotland and be a crofter . . . raise sheep, raise children, live like my ancestors, free men, happy men—"

Jody froze at the head of the stairs, watching him. There was such intensity in his voice, such misery in his face, as he stared out over the water, it broke her heart. "Eric?" she whispered.

His face jerked around to meet hers, and then he shrugged. "Forget it, Jody. I'm fine."

"Are you sure?"

"Yes," he answered. "I'm okay. Go get dressed, and I'll take us up the coast . . . or west toward Marquesas Keys or the Dry Tortugas. Ever been there?"

"I've never been anywhere. I'd love to go to the Tortugas with you, Mr. Ransom, mustache or no mustache."

"What?" His hand went to his upper lip, and he gave a short bark of laughter. "Stupid thing.

Soon as we hit open water, I'll take the damn thing off and give you a good-morning kiss you won't forget."

"Oh, promises, promises." Laughing softly to herself, she went below to shower and dress.

"This is what I like, a well-stocked ship," Jody announced, emerging on deck a half hour later in a two-piece red bathing suit.

The water was churning into white foam behind them, the boat cutting smoothly through the turquoise waters of the Gulf.

Eric turned his gaze from the sea, and his eyebrows shot up in appreciation. "Nice," he said.

"There was also a string bikini in the locker I found this in, but I flushed it down the toilet."

"Head," he corrected automatically, staring at her. "And you didn't really, did you?"

"No, but *I'm* not going to wear it. And since no one else is allowed on board from now on who might possibly need to borrow a bathing suit from you, or have a body good enough to wear *that* one . . . well, it might as well get tossed, right?"

A smile tugged at the corner of his mouth. "Feeling pretty feisty now, aren't we?"

Jody blushed and bit her lip. She walked over behind him and rested her cheek on his back. "Am I awful? Am I going too far, too fast?"

Eric pulled her around in front of him and kissed her. "No. You're just perfect, Jody. Perfect."

"Are you sure? I warned you, I do tend to get carried away. If I'm sure I'm right, I go for it; and next thing you know, there I am with mud on my face or my foot in my mouth. And I'm always surprised. You'd think I'd learn—" She let her hands fall open, as if even now surprised that she hadn't.

"We all make mistakes."

"But I keep telling myself to go slowly, watch my step. Don't follow *every* damn impulse."

"But I like your impulses," he teased, chasing away her frown.

"You're sure?" She looked deep into his eyes, needing reassurance.

"Absolutely. All of them. Every last one . . . from the tip of your nose"—he kissed her there, playfully but nice—"to the tip of your toes. And every one in between."

How could he make her feel so womanly and so girlish all at the same time? It was amazing, and wonderful.

She kissed him back, sliding her tongue oh-so-slowly across his bottom lip.

A satisfying rumble of laughter rose in his chest, and she could see the goose bumps rise across his skin. She moved her mouth slowly to the side and blew in his ear, grinning when he shivered. Then she slipped her tongue in his ear and took a quick nip at his earlobe.

"Hey! Cut that out or we'll never get anywhere today."

"Suits me fine," she purred into his ear. "I'm happy right here, doing exactly what I'm doing."

"But I thought you wanted to explore."

"I *am* exploring, you foolish man," she teased.

"Wait a minute. I thought you just told me you were going to stop being so impulsive," he whispered, though he didn't sound as though he meant a word of it.

It gave Jody a surge of excitement that was as strong as arousal. She could make him sound like this, could make his head fall languidly to one side, his eyes half-closed, his breath coming quick. Oh, the delight of having such power. The thrill! It made her wild and reckless.

She slipped her hands down over his shoulders and across his back, then drew her nails lightly across his skin. He shuddered, and she shivered with delight. She pressed her mouth to the ridge of muscle that capped his shoulder and drew her tongue along his skin. He was salty, warm, delicious.

He took one hand off the steering wheel and reached up, trying to capture her, but she slipped away, unwilling to be caught.

"No, no. You have to steer the boat. You're in charge of getting us away from here, remember?"

"Suddenly, I don't remember a thing."

"We're going to the Tortugas, remember, to a spot where no one can find us? A place with no Peeping Toms. A special place, a secret place."

"We are?"

"Yes. So you keep steering the boat, and I'll take care of . . . of whiling the time away, okay?"

"You keep whiling the time away *that* way, and

we're not going anywhere but to bed." He cut the engine to idle.

"Ummmm, what a nice idea. I like the way your mind works, Mr. Ransom. But first, you have a job to do."

"I can't with you here . . . with you touching me like that, Ms. Conners."

"Like this, you mean? Is that a problem?" she whispered, her hands moving slowly over his skin. She added wistfully, "Well, then, I'll just have to sit down over there and act demure."

"No. Please. Anything but that," he said with mock panic. "Here, do me a favor. Hold the wheel for a minute."

"Why?"

"Just do it." He took both her hands and put them on the steering wheel, then slid off the seat. In a minute he had peeled off his shorts and dove naked as a jaybird off the side rail and into the water.

"Wait!" she yelped. "Come back! What do I do?" She did the first thing she could think of: She switched off the engine.

The boat rocked to a stop, then kept on rocking in the gentle current of the Gulf of Mexico.

"Eric?" she shouted.

"I'm right here." He startled her when his voice came from the opposite side of the boat. He was about twenty feet away, floating shamelessly on his back, grinning at her.

"You rascal! Get back here!"

"And face such torture? Such torment? Never!" He took a mouthful of water and spit it high into the air like a whale. Without a splash he did a neat, quick surface dive and came up just at the rail.

"Come on in; the water's fine."

She lifted her chin in disdain. "How? The boat'll float away."

"Go drop anchor. It's shallow here. Go ahead . . . then come on in. I have something to show you."

"What? A fish?" She peered down over the rail at him, right there below, all tan and glistening. "Hmmm? Is that a fish you want to show me? An eel?"

His laughter echoed across the water. "Come find out."

Jody clambered awkwardly up onto the narrow edge of the boat, then around to the prow. With a grunt she hefted the anchor and tossed it overboard. Wiping her hands on her thighs, she climbed back down, then leaned over the rail.

He was right there, waiting, grinning.

"So, you think this'll be worth my while? I mean, getting wet and all—"

"I'd sure like you to give it a try, Ms. Conners," he drawled.

Frantic with desire, she put one bare foot on the rail. "Watch out then." And with a splash she jumped in.

When she came up, he was waiting, all wet, hungry mouth and hands and skin, all slippery and slick, all smooth and polished.

Kisses tasted of salt. Lips slid easily; tongues darted like fish.

Each caress was heightened by the warmth of the water, its fluid surge and rush over every inch of her skin. The water and his hands became indistinguishable. A touch here, a touch there . . . moving across her flesh, never ceasing, stirring her like a frond of seaweed, like a sea anemone, touching her, filling her.

She caught him around the neck and clung to him. She wrapped her legs around his hips and let herself move with him, riding the currents, lifting and falling. She relinquished the nearness of the boat, the sandy bottom just below, the sun up above. There was only him, only Eric, in all the wild, wide sea.

When she came, she pressed her mouth into the flesh of his shoulder, not willing to let a sound escape, not wanting to stop, not wanting it ever to end.

Eric held her tight, his own body still racked by shudders. He pushed his face into her hair. "I've never done that before."

"Me neither, but it was wonderful." Satisfied and utterly relaxed, she released her hold on his neck, leaned back, and let the water take her.

She sighed, floating lightly on the surface of the water. "This is wonderful."

"And much easier," he added.

She splashed water in his face. "What a thing to say when I'm feeling so romantic," she scolded.

"Sorry . . . sorry . . ." But his voice was unrepentant. He floated away, almost out of sight, only his feet still within touching distance. So she touched one; she couldn't resist.

He wiggled his toes in silent communion.

Jody smiled up at the sunlit sky, the perfect cotton-ball clouds. She had never been so happy. Never knew it was possible to be so happy. Never even dreamed it.

A moment passed, then another, and then there was a slight ruffle of water, the tiniest waves breaking over her breasts. Eric's foot slipped from her hand. His hand curved under the back of her head.

When she opened her eyes, he was blocking the sun.

"If we don't get going, we'll never make it to the Tortugas today."

"I don't care," she said simply. "I really don't."

"I thought I'd show you the birds, the turtles. . . ."

"Another time, maybe? I'm happy here."

"Are you?"

"Yes. I am. I'm happier than I've ever been. I don't want to go sightseeing."

"Sure?"

"Oh yes. I am absolutely positive." But when she lowered her feet and stood *up*, her head spun. "Then again, maybe it is time to get back on deck."

"Come on." He let her swim ahead, then gave her a boost up to the rail. "Got it?" he called.

"Yes, I'm fine." She reached a hand down to him, and in moments they were wrapped in thick terry-cloth towels, sitting on the deck, backs against the rail. His feet stuck out past hers, and she tickled his ankle with her big toe.

"Eric Ransom, you are something else."

"What?" he asked, draping his arm around her shoulder. "What exactly am I?"

"A wonderful man. A tender, passionate man. Everything . . . absolutely everything I ever dreamed of."

Above them, the sun swung in an arc from east to west. Hours passed while they talked and laughed, or sat silently, thinking their own thoughts.

"You know what?" asked Jody, rubbing her palm across Eric's chest. "I wish I had a present to give you. Don't shake your head no, I mean it. I wish I had something fantastic to give you. A surprise. Something that would take your breath away!"

"*You* take my breath away, Ms. Conners. That's enough of a surprise."

She smiled and snuggled up against him. "Good. But I still wish . . ." She bit her lower lip, staring up into the cloudless sky as if a sign would appear. She tipped her head, frowned, thought some more. "When we get home, I could cook you something. They do say the way to a man's heart is through his stomach."

"They do, huh? And what exactly would you make me?"

"Let's see. Moo shu pork in delicate little pancakes, thin as silk, speckled golden brown and melting on your tongue?"

"Interesting."

"Okay . . . how about Kan shao beef? It's hot, spicy, and irresistible."

"Sounds like you, my little temptress," he said, brushing her cheek with the back of his fingers.

Jody grinned. "Then I'll make you spareribs. Basted in soy and honey, mmm, so sticky and yummy . . . and it'll run down your fingers, and you'll have to lick them off . . . like this. . . ." She caught his hand and brought it to her lips.

"Cut that out," he admonished as he pressed against her and lowered her to the deck. "Oh, you do make an afternoon pass nicely, Ms. Conners. I can't remember ever feeling this . . . this . . ." He shrugged, at a loss for the right word until his eyes met hers. Then he smiled. " . . . this content. Relaxed. At peace."

Jody felt her heart swell. Happiness bloomed inside her, opening petal by petal until it filled her soul.

"I know exactly what you mean, Eric," she whispered. "I always keep so busy, with the school, the children, orders, repairs, meetings, that sometimes I could cry, I'm so tired. But then, when I'm alone, I hurry up and find something else to do. I'm always so *restless*. . . ." She, too, struggled to find the right words; it seemed so important now. "It's always been as though I'm both running *to* something, and *away* from it at the same time. Never content. Until now. This moment . . . here with you."

He lay silently beside her for a long moment, staring up at the sky until his eyes watered. "Can it last?" he asked.

Jody leaned over him, hands pressed firmly into his shoulder muscles, her whole weight pinning him to the deck. She kissed him hard on the mouth instead of answering, because she had no answer to give him.

At night there were a million, million stars sparkling overhead. The Milky Way was a luminous glow, bright and close enough to dip your hands in and scatter like jewels across the Gulf. Jody counted three shooting stars, though Eric insisted the last was a UFO.

"Little green men are going to land and get us," she joked, nibbling happily on cheese and crackers.

"No," he shouted, waving them off with a grand gesture. "Yesterday, okay. But not today. Not now. I'm too happy here."

"I second that," Jody said, lifting her wineglass in a toast. "Here's to being happy."

Eric put his glass down, untasted. His face had gone pale.

"What is it?" Jody asked, reaching out to touch his cheek.

"Nothing." He was breathing hard through parted lips, his chest rising and falling. "It's nothing. A sudden reality attack." He shook his head, mute, hurting, but when he looked up and met her eyes, he forced a smile. "It's okay, Jody. We'll figure it out as we go along. Don't worry."

"I'm not worried. I know we'll work it out . . . somehow."

"Yeah." He narrowed his eyes. "You could come live here—"

"That wouldn't work. *You* don't like living here, I know it despite what you say. Hiding away. Living on their terms," she said softly, stroking his cheek. "I can't bear to see you hurting. Somehow, somehow, we'll figure it out, Eric." The look she gave him was full of desperate hope . . . fragile, tenuous.

With great effort he emptied his face, steadying his breathing. "You're right," he said, smiling at her. "It will all be fine. Come here to me."

The next morning Jody woke up talking. She had to tell Eric about her family, her parents, her childhood up in Atlanta; about tubing down the Chattahoochee with her sister and summer camp in North Carolina; about the children in her class last year and those who were now in third grade, her first "graduating" class and how she and Anne had made little mortarboards with tassels for them all to wear, but Stevie Lipschutz cried and cried and wouldn't wear his.

She listed her favorite books, her favorite music, all the places she hoped to visit someday, the worst experiences of her life. She laid it all out there on the deck of the boat in the morning sun, compelled to talk on and on until he knew her, really knew her. Compelled to bind them to each other, tighter and

tighter. The words working to push the fear
away . . .

"Tell me more," he'd say whenever she stopped
to catch her breath.

She was lying on the deck now, her head in
his lap, and he was absentmindedly brushing his
fingers through her hair, watching her with that
dark, intent gaze of his.

He meant to listen. At first he had, concen-
trating on every word, picturing the life she
described. But now his mind was drifting. The
heat of her against his thighs, the silkiness of
her hair, the scent of her sun-warmed skin,
filled his senses, and his mind floated aloft
like a lazy balloon, drifting on the current of
her words.

But his being, the heart of him, was entirely
focused. In the deepest, most intimate sense his
soul was communing with hers.

This moment, here within the narrow confines
of the boat, was the happiest moment he'd ever
known. This woman, fresh as dew, sweet as honey, was a miracle who had somehow fallen from
above and landed in his lap. The years of hiding,
the years of loneliness, seemed bearable now . . .
now that he could put them behind him. It
frightened him to think how lonely he had been.
How angry, how wary. How the black moods had
swept over him. Frightened him more to think of
the future. How? Where? But how could he ever
live without her now? *Oh God—*

No! He wouldn't think of that. He unclenched

his hand and gently brushed the hair away from her cheek, then rubbed a strand between his fingers. This, this was enough: this day, this woman. If it was all he had of happiness, it would have to be enough. Somehow.

"Pardon?"

"What? Oh . . . nothing . . ." He blushed, realizing he must have spoken aloud. "Nothing, dear one. Go on . . . tell me more."

A storm blew in from the south that evening, and they sat way back under the canvas top, cuddled in each other's arms, eating olives and asparagus spears straight from the cans, watching the waves lift and dance.

"It's a lot more fun here than on that stupid raft," Jody said, shaking her head at the memory.

"When I think what could have happened to you—" he broke off, frowning, swallowing hard, " . . . I can't stand it."

"But look at what *did* happen," she insisted, rubbing his frown away with her fingertips, then pulling his face close. "Look what magic did occur!" She kissed him, parting her lips to taste him, tantalize him.

He backhanded the cans into the corner and drew her down on the deck, covering every inch of her with his muscular frame. "Not getting wet, are you?" he asked, worried about the weather.

"I am," she answered feeling delightfully naughty, "but not because of the rain."

He replied to her invitation with a seductive grin, and soon they were both oblivious to everything except the rhythms of their own two bodies joining as one.

Ten

"I guess we'd better be heading back," Eric said the next afternoon.

"Oh, just another few minutes? A few hours? A few *days*? Please?"

"Only minutes." But he sat where he was, his arm around her shoulder. His eyes traveled the horizon, then came back to her face.

Jody had her eyes closed, and he studied her closely, intently, as if memorizing every feature. He lifted his hand and touched her eyelashes with one finger, then traced her brow. She smiled under his touch, blinked, opened her eyes.

"I'm still awake."

"I know. I just wanted to touch you."

"I know."

He let his head drop back against the polished wood, eyes closed, but only for a moment. "We really have to go. We've got a few hours of sailing ahead, and I'd rather not be taking her in among the groves in the dark without some help."

"Couldn't we have just one more swim?" Jody asked, desperately trying to keep time from moving on. "One more kiss? One more you-know-what?"

"Only the kiss." He lowered his face to hers, letting his tongue press open her lips and seek hers. They kissed for a long moment, hands on each other's shoulders.

"I can't talk you into one more day?" Jody whispered.

"There's not enough fuel. Not enough to eat."

"Oh, we could live on love."

"I really don't want to go either," he said softly.

"I know," she answered, brushing her lips back and forth across the stubble on his chin. "But you're right. I don't know a thing about boats. I won't be much help in the dark."

"You'll be fine." He gave her a quick, fierce kiss, then pushed her away. "You can start by pulling anchor while I run the bilge for a minute and check the running lights, just in case we need them later. Okay?"

On the way home they were going against the current, and the ride was slow and rolling. Up one swell and down again, up and down, with the engine humming. Behind them clouds gathered and darkened on the horizon. The wind picked up.

Jody had pulled on a sweatshirt she found below. Eric still stood at the wheel, bare-chested, his jeans hung low on his lean hips. They shared a beer and ate chocolate bars and crackers for a late lunch. The sun moved across the sky, warming her hair, turning the skin on his back to bronze. Jody had no restraint left; she touched him when she wanted to, where she wanted to: his shoulder blades, his spine, the small of his back, his neck.

"Chilly?" she asked.

"I could use a shirt."

"I'll get you one."

She brought him back an old, faded sweatshirt and held the wheel while he put it on.

"Who usually goes out with you for company? Or shouldn't I ask?"

"You can ask me anything, my love. Matthew usually comes with me. We fish. We take the boat down to Fort Jeff—that's the Dry Tortugas—and dive the coral reefs. Or we go salvaging."

"What's that?"

"Diving for wrecks. Old Spanish galleons. Pirate ships and treasure. They're all over the place down here. It's all rocks and shallow waters between Key West and Fort Jeff."

"Do you ever find any?"

"Ships, yes, but no treasure, not yet. But it is exciting."

"I'd like to go."

"I bet you would," he said. "But I'd have to teach you how to dive first. You'd need to be certified. You have to know the rules, the consequences. It's not just all fun."

"Oh, why so serious? I sort of figured I'd put on a wet suit and jump right in. I've watched Jacques Cousteau on TV, you know."

He looked at her, knowing she was teasing but feeling compelled to answer sharply. "Jody, some things you have to be completely serious about, or you put yourself in danger."

When she stared at him, he colored and looked away. "I'm sorry. I don't know what's bothering me." He shrugged, frowning out at the sea ahead. "Shoot, I wish we weren't going back."

"Then let's not," she said quickly, her soul at one with his. She slipped her arms around his neck. There was a sudden chill in the air, and she pressed herself tightly against him, trying to hide there. "Let's just keep going, Eric. Somewhere. Anywhere!"

He held her close and whispered in her hair. "We have to go back, Jody. It would be too dangerous. Besides, there are some things you can't ignore, things you can't run away from. . . . But it will be all right."

"Of course it will," she said, more loudly than she intended. She leaned back against the circle of his arms. "Of course it will. What a silly thing to say." She shivered, a chill walking her arms and neck. "Oh, that wind! I hate that wind."

The wind chased them in to shore. It moaned and whispered among the mangroves, and the mangroves tugged at their roots. The roots groaned, or so Jody thought, listening to them in the gathering darkness. Once there was a huge splash just off to the right of the boat as a big gator, twelve feet from eyeballs to tail, slid off a log into the murky water. Jody jumped.

"Good thing we're almost there," he said. "You look exhausted."

"I am," she admitted, snuggling closer to his side.

"Well, another thirty minutes and we'll be home. Lena's good cooking, your own soft bed. No more wooden deck to sleep on—"

"But I loved sleeping on the deck with you. It was wonderful."

"Yes, it was," he agreed, his voice resonant in the darkness. He caught himself and added lightly, "And now a hot shower will feel mighty good too."

"I guess so . . . though it doesn't seem like a fair trade."

"Jody—" he began, but he turned away so that she could no longer see his face. "Jody, we'll have to go more slowly now. We have to deal with the real world—"

Jody wanted to say, "To hell with the real world! I want to sail away with you forever! I'll even hide away with you here behind this bramble hedge for a hundred years, and no one will come to wake us! I'll do *anything* to have you, to sleep with you, to love you. . . ."

She wanted to say it. But she couldn't.

She thought, *You* say it, Eric, say it for me please, right out loud.

Instead, he said, "Why don't we just take it one thing at a time, Jody, okay?" That was all.

The silence lengthened with the dusk. She couldn't see his face clearly, couldn't read his eyes. The night was a mask that dropped over his face, and he was hidden behind it. Suddenly, she felt unsure of herself, as rocky as the boat weaving its way through the dense, stubborn mangroves.

Then all at once the pier was there, and the house just beyond it, lights shining in the windows. It looked so big as they came upon it suddenly in the dark, sprawling and exotic. She realized she hadn't seen any of it but the kitchen, her room, the stairway in between. It was a disconcerting thought. Had she really been here for such a short time? Known him for such a short time?

She wanted to touch him, needed to touch him, but she felt shy, inexplicably frightened.

"Eric? . . ." she began, then hesitated.

"What?"

Stop! Don't land! her soul cried, but she dared not say it. She knew he'd think her foolish, impulsive and silly. She knew that in reality what she desired *was* all those things. And that they were impossible. She bit her lip, tasting blood.

"What is it, Jody?"

"Nothing. I . . . I was going to ask if you needed me to help dock, but here we are."

"Yes, here we are." Without another look he grabbed on to the piling with one hand. With the other he cut the engine, then he leapt up onto the rail, then the pier, and looped the heavy rope around the piling, tying it off in a square knot. Neat. Perfect. Finished.

He gave Jody a hand up, then jumped back down on deck to check the instruments, turn off the lights, snap the heavy canvas cover over the deck.

Jody stood on the pier, one arm wrapped around the piling, watching him work. Oh, how she loved this man! It was inconceivable that he would not always be part of her life. Surely, surely . . . if she was the puzzle, he was the answer.

In the darkness she drew a deep breath, and smiled.

Eric looked up and saw her smiling in the moonlight. He smiled back up at her. "Done in a second," he said.

"No hurry," she answered. "I'm fine. It's a beautiful night, isn't it?"

He looked at her. "Yes. Very beautiful."

"We're back!" Eric called, pulling open the screen door with one hand, his other tight around Jody's waist.

Matthew scraped back his kitchen chair and stood. "Hoped you'd be home this evening. Lena's made the best bouillabaisse I've ever tasted. Outdone herself!"

"Why, I thank you, Matthew." From over near the stove Lena welcomed the returning pair with a smile. "That is what I call good timing. The smell of these biscuits must have brought you home. Sit on down, and I'll set you both a place."

"I'll help, Lena," Jody said quickly, heading for the cupboard. But Lena blocked her way. "You, girl, look like you are going to fall over. Sit yourself down and be a guest for one more night; tomorrow I'll let you help."

"Deal," Jody said gratefully.

"So," Matthew said in that deep, soft voice of his, "did you see where the herons nest?"

Jody and Eric looked at each other, their eyes locking across the distance.

"We'll have to do that tomorrow," Eric said softly.

Matthew discreetly turned his attention to his bouillabaisse.

It was long past midnight. Jody lay in bed, willing sleep to come fetch her. She counted sheep. Hummed lullabies. Replayed scenes from the past days and nights on the boat . . . but that only made things worse.

"For heaven's sake," she growled, punching her pillow into a fluffy ball. "I've got to get some sleep."

Instead, she tossed and turned. Every sense was keen, alert. Had she heard someone edging past her door? Did she smell late-night coffee brewing? Was there a cure for the fire licking its way up from her belly, spreading hot along her limbs?

She could imagine the cure to *all* her problems, could conjure him up in the flower-scented darkness: Eric Ransom. He was both cause and cure of this unbearable desire, this yearning, this need.

Eric, who had so calmly and inexplicably said good night at the foot of the stairs and now must be sound asleep in his own bed, oblivious to her very existence. How could he do that? Would she ever sleep again?

She groaned and rolled over, burying her head under her pillow. But a sudden thought pursued her there: *Heaven helps those who help themselves.*

Climbing out of bed, she pulled a light robe over the T-shirt she was sleeping in. She brushed her teeth again, and her hair. She went to the door and put her hand on the knob. Did she dare? Heck, what did she have to lose?

Tiptoeing out into the hall, she pulled the door shut behind her without a sound. Then she stopped.

She didn't have the vaguest idea where Eric's room was, upstairs or down, this side of the house or the other. Not a clue.

A shadow detached itself from the dark end of the hall, making her jump. "Eric?"

"Shhh," he whispered, placing a finger on her lips. He grabbed her hand and led her down the stairs. She floated behind him, her feet never touching the ground.

He led her away from the kitchen, down a long hallway, through a door, and into a moonlit room. There were a desk where a small lamp had been left burning, a couch and some chairs.

French doors had been thrown open wide to the night air. Another door in the far wall stood half-open, beckoning.

Still not speaking, Eric led her on through the second door into his bedroom. The covers on the bed were thrown back, the pillows propped against the headboard, the sheets in tangled disarray.

Releasing her hand, he took a step away and folded his arms across his chest. "I give up. I can't sleep without you," he said. His voice was rough and irritable in the darkness. "I tried. I can't. My bones ache, my muscles are in knots. I'm walking the halls in my own house on tiptoe, sneaking around like some thief." He heaved a sigh of defeat. "Common sense be damned! Sleep with me, will you?"

Jody nodded quickly, afraid to speak. She curved herself against the now-familiar lines of his body. "Yes, yes . . . a thousand times yes," she whispered, sliding her hands under his shirt.

"Wait," he said, catching hold of her wrists. "None of that. We've got to slow down a little. Now that we've got our feet on solid ground—"

She covered his mouth with hers, stealing his breath away. As she kissed him, she ran her hands over his skin, slowly, starting at his back and moving around his ribs.

"Wait! I'm serious, Jody. Let me be serious for a minute. Cut that out and listen to me. We've got to start dealing with reality, like it or not. We've got to think ahead. . . . But I'm so damn tired, if I don't get some sleep, I'm gonna fall over. So come lie down beside me for tonight, but no fooling around. None."

"Whatever you say," she breathed. "I'll agree to any terms. Any."

"Then if *I* don't make the first move. . . ."

". . . . *what* could you possibly have to fear?"

He looked at her, his soul warring between necessity and desire. The battle shone in his dark, smoldering eyes. Then, furious at his own weakness, he surrendered and led her to the bed. He straightened the sheets and held the cover up for her.

Jody slid under, trembling with joy.

Eric slid in beside her and pulled the covers up over their shoulders. He gave her one warning look, his dark eyes burning in the moonlight, then switched off the lamp.

Jody wiggled over next to him.

He turned on his side, his back to her.

She draped an arm over his arm, her hand falling against his chest.

He made a small sound in the darkness.

She slid her hand down to his belly. "Sorry," she whispered. "I was just getting comfortable."

"Then *get* comfortable, and lie still. Please!"

"I'm trying," she said earnestly.

He growled something, pushing his head into the pillow.

"Am I crowding you?" she asked, raising onto one elbow and swaying, dizzy with the nearness of him, the heat, the lust, the overwhelming desire.

"No . . . you're fine, if you'll just go to sleep."

"Okay, just checking." Settling back down, she happened to press her breasts against his back.

"Jody! Are you doing this on purpose?"

"Sorry, sorry. See, I *am* crowding you. Sorry." As she readjusted her position, her arm happened to slip down over his hip, her hand grazing his manhood.

He stirred, hardening. "Oh, heaven help me," he moaned, his breath rattling in his throat. "Jody—"

"Yes?" she asked, her breath warm on his cheek.

He caught her in his arms and settled her down on top of him. "What would your fairy tales have to say about this, my love?"

"They always end with just a kiss, so we'll have to wing it on our own."

Eleven

Morning came too soon.

Jody would have stayed in bed for days, for *years*, happy just to watch Eric lying beside her, or dripping wet from his shower, or standing naked in front of the mirror as he shaved.

But he tossed her out of bed, insisting there were things to be done today.

She fussed and dawdled but finally tied on her robe and followed him into the ordinary morning light of the kitchen.

"Sleep well?" Lena asked.

"Fine, thanks."

"Yes, just fine," Jody echoed.

"I'm glad to hear it," Lena assured them. "Me, I thought I heard all kinda noises out in the hall in the middle of the night."

"Must have been mice," Eric said, the picture of absolute innocence.

Jody hid her burning cheeks behind her napkin.

Lena, nonplussed, served coffee, croissants, and mango preserves. Watching Jody nibble at a corner of a croissant, she offered omelets, pancakes, homemade granola with dates and almonds.

Jody saw herself shake her head and murmur a polite refusal. She felt suspended, adrift at a distance, floating like one of the millions of dust motes caught in the sunbeams pouring through the kitchen window. Eating was the last thing on her mind.

Matthew came in just in time to join them for a second cup, and his noise was a welcome distraction. "Morning, ladies, Eric. Any problems with the boat?"

"None," Eric answered, stretching up and folding his arms behind his head. "She handled beautifully. You did a good job on the bilge pump. Thanks."

"No problem."

"She does need to be fueled before we take her out again."

"I'll take care of that right after breakfast. By the way, did Lena tell you Chandler's message from New York? There's still trouble with the landlord over at the theater. No air-conditioning. He hasn't fixed the wiring in the prop room. And last Thursday and Friday there wasn't any water."

"Damn," Eric swore, shaking his head in disgust. "Real helpful son of a gun, isn't he? You know what, go ahead and buy the building. It's a great space, good location. We've talked about it—we might as well just get it done."

"Sounds fine."

"Anything else?"

"I'm taking the skiff up to town later to shop," Lena interrupted. "Anything special you're hungry for?"

"Not me," Eric said with a shrug, looking across at Jody. "How about you?"

"No thanks," she answered quickly. "I've got everything *I* want."

Damned if Eric didn't blush, the blood rising quickly across his throat.

Matthew stared in surprise. "So . . . ah, do you want the boat ready for this afternoon?"

Eric ignored the look, struggling to keep his own face stern. "No rush. I'm going to take Jody over and show her where the herons nest."

"Sure," Matthew drawled, folding his napkin and giving Lena a wink across the kitchen. "We've heard that one before, haven't we? Then you two don't show up for days!"

"These things happen," Eric said, a grin tugging at the corner of his mouth. "We just went a little farther than we expected."

"So we guessed."

The herons nested on the mangrove islands just south of the house. At the first footsteps the huge birds took to the sky, heads drawn back, their flight slow and laborious. Their harsh, loud cries broke the silence.

"Oh, we frightened them," Jody said guiltily.

"Don't worry, they'll be back. They've got eggs in the nests."

"They're beautiful. And so big! I never dreamed they were so big."

"Audubon called them the 'angels of the swamps.' Nice, huh?"

"Wonderful. You show me the most wonderful things. Can we sit down and watch till they come back?"

"Better not. The mosquitoes will get us." Even as he said it, one landed on the bare skin of his forearm. He flattened it with a slap. "Come on—we can take the canoe out a little ways and maybe get a look at them from the other side without getting eaten alive."

"Whatever you say," she agreed, slapping at her neck and then her right calf. "Yikes, they're after me!"

They ran down to the pier. Eric helped Jody into the prow, handed her a paddle and a life jacket, and climbed in behind her. Calling directions, he guided the canoe out through the mangroves and into the open. The warm green waters of the Gulf lay flat around them, ironed smooth by a breathless heat.

"Whew . . . not a breeze. No wonder the bugs're so bad."

Jody dipped a hand overboard and dripped water down her neck. "Maybe we should go back."

"I'd rather be alone with you."

She smiled. "Could we take the boat back

out and go visit the Dry Tortugas? See Fort Jefferson? Look for treasure?"

"I want to talk."

"We can talk as we ride." She wiggled her brows at him.

"Oh, no. The *last* thing we'd end up doing is talking."

"And the first?"

"You know darn well."

"And what's so bad about *that*?" she demanded, the spark, so quickly ignited, burning away her reticence.

"Jody, we *need* to talk."

She lifted her paddle out of the water and half turned on the seat to face him. Waited a heartbeat. "Uh-oh. I don't like the way that sounds, Mr. Ransom," she said softly. Shading her face with the flat of one hand, she looked into his face. "I don't think I want to do this."

"We have to."

"Why?" she insisted. "Why can't we just enjoy the morning, the time together?"

He looked at her, the paddle hanging forgotten from one hand. "How long have you been here, Jody?"

The question surprised her. "Oh, I don't know." She shrugged. "I've been too busy to count. Maybe a week?"

"Eighteen days," he said softly. "I found you eighteen days ago."

"What?" Her mouth fell open. Her heart

stopped. Her mind spun. "No! That can't be right. It can't be."

"It is. So there are things we have to do. First, why don't we have Lena send a telegram for you from Everglades City? Let your partner know you're delayed. Get someone else to go in."

"There *is* no one else," she snapped. "There's just the two of us. I told you that. We do *everything*, all of it!" Her voice rose with her frustration. Tears welled, blurring her sight. "Damn! Oh Eric, Eric . . . what are we going to do?"

He reached across the space between them, making the canoe rock. "Hey, don't cry. We'll figure it out. Hey . . . Jody, we'll work it out. Don't cry. Please."

"But what will happen to us? Oh, Eric . . ." She took his hand and pressed her face against his palm. Closing her eyes, she breathed in the smell of him, the warmth.

I won't go back. I don't want to go back. . . .

The chant ran through her head, chasing away rational thought. Behind it came a dull roar that filled her ears, the roar of her blood pounding in fear, and the dark grip of a blinding headache.

She felt Eric slip his hand from hers and loosen her fingers from the paddle. She felt the canoe rock as he returned to his place in the stern, felt the slide of the canoe across the water and the measured pull of his strokes, the resisting tug of the water.

She kept her eyes closed, her hands pressed to her temples, fighting a migraine.

When they reached shore, he dragged the boat

up as far as he could on the sandy bottom and knelt in the bottom of the canoe, holding her. "Jody, it'll be all right. You'll stay here with me. We'll work it out—"

But it was like talking to a statue. Jody sat, head bent against the front of his shirt, weeping, getting eaten by mosquitoes and too immobilized even to brush them away. The constant whine of the insects was the only sound breaking the silence.

Then the whole canoe shook as he slammed the side with his paddle. "Dammit!" he shouted. He threw the paddle down and lifted her right out of her seat. "Come on. You're coming with me."

He pulled her up the path toward the house, already yelling instructions ahead. "Matthew, throw some extra blankets on the boat. Pillows. Clothes. Lena, pack sandwiches. Something to drink."

Lena and Matthew met them at the kitchen door. "What's happened? Are you all right? What's going on?"

"No questions. Just hurry."

They read the expression on his face and turned, then disappeared. In moments they were back.

Eric eyed the supplies and nodded. "Thanks. Matthew, did you fuel the boat?"

"She's ready to go. Restocked the galley. Fresh towels too."

"Thank you. I'm taking her out." He held the door open for Jody, and when she didn't move, he pushed her through. "Don't wait dinner. We won't be back."

"Ever?" Lena asked softly.

Eric paused for a minute and caught his breath. A muscle jumped along his jaw. "Not tonight. You both take care. Thanks."

He didn't give Jody a chance to say a word. Which was just fine with her; she was speechless, overwhelmed with emotion.

Once they set foot on the boat, the trance seemed broken; she started to function again.

She knew how to push the stern away from the pilings as the boat left the pier.

She stowed the supplies below in the cabin.

She settled back on the bench seat next to the captain's chair and watched Eric's hands on the wheel.

The mangroves slid away. The island vanished. Open water surrounded them. He headed straight out, straight west into the open Gulf, pushing the boat to top speed. They flew over the water, their wake rising and curling behind them, the engine drowning out all other sound.

Eric drove like that for an hour. Silent. Intent. Staring ahead through the windshield.

Jody gave herself up to the whip of the wind, the splatter of spray, the roar of the motor. She kept her eyes on the far horizon and her head full of meaningless noise. An hour.

Then, all at once, the engine hushed; the boat stopped its headlong dash and settled back into its own wake.

"Don't say anything," he warned.

She shook her head.

He took off all his clothes until he stood before her naked, beautiful, his body gleaming with salt spray and sweat.

She stood and took off her clothes, dropping them in a pile at her feet.

He touched her cheek, her nipples, the dark triangle of curly hair.

She stepped into his embrace, fitting her body to his, pressing herself into his flesh until they merged and became one.

They made love standing up, leaning against the back of the captain's chair when her knees started to buckle.

Afterward, he slowly pulled free of her arms and stood at the rail, looking down at the water, head bowed.

"I love you, Eric," she whispered.

"And I love you. I want you to stay with me."

Jody covered her eyes with one hand. "Oh, Eric, God knows I want to be with you, that's the truth! But not . . . not hiding away here. Eric . . ." She leaned up against him, circling him from behind with her arms, her cheek pressed warm against his shoulder blade. "Eric? Won't you come back with me?"

"No!" He stiffened, then turned around, the blood draining from his face. "I can't. You *have* to understand that. You have to believe me. It's up to you. Just say you'll stay, Jody . . . that's all you've got to do."

She started to cry silently, and he tenderly kissed each tear rolling down her cheeks.

"Jody . . . Jody, don't do this." He shook his head, his eyes red-rimmed and burning.

"Eric, I have to go—"

"No," he groaned. "No." He kissed her eyes, her throat, her breasts. "Say you won't leave me—"

She clung to him, shaking, casting about wildly for the right word, for *any* words to explain. "Eric, I love you. I do. But this is not the way. I can't stay. And you shouldn't—"

"I have to. And you could if you loved me enough."

"I love you more than that. Enough to want to keep you from living your life like this, on other people's terms. Hiding. Cutting yourself off from the world, from life. No! You're too brave for that. Too wonderful."

He grabbed her, pulling her up hard against him. "I don't want flattery. I want *you*, Jody. Here. Now. Forever."

"It wouldn't work, Eric. It wouldn't be good for us, for the two of us together. You know that in your heart. And though it breaks my heart to see you in pain, I have to convince you—"

"*You're* going to convince *me*?" He was yelling now, at the edge of his self-control. "You? The one who believes in fairy tales and magic? You're going to tell *me* how to deal with reality?"

"Eric, you make it sound so . . . awful. So impossible. It isn't! Trust me—"

"How can I? If you can leave me that easily, how can I trust you?"

"That's a terrible thing to say. I can't believe you said that, Eric."

"Believe it!" he snarled.

"Don't do this, Eric. *Please*. Stop it. Look at me. Listen to me: I love you, and we'll work it out. And while I'm away, I'll keep your secret—"

"But you'll go now and leave me alone here?" he asked, his voice rough and breaking. "You'd take away my company, my happiness? You'd leave me alone again, with no one to love?"

She stared at him openmouthed, stunned. "Eric . . ." Tears choked her, and she swallowed against them, needing to find words, the right words. "Eric, we'll find the answer. Together. That's the best I—"

He pushed her away and strode to the captain's chair. "Then go."

"What?"

"You heard me. Just go. As a matter of fact, I'll take you right now."

Leaping onto the prow, he pulled up the anchor and threw it on the deck, sending paint chips flying. In a minute he was at the wheel, revving the engine. The boat lurched forward. Jody had to grab on to the back of one of the fishing chairs to keep from falling.

"Stop it!" she yelled, struggling to his side. Reaching wildly across him, she hit at the throttle. The boat slowed. "Stop this, Eric! Listen—"

He turned to her, his face cold as stone. "What?"

She was afraid to touch him, afraid to speak. But she had to. "Eric," she said softly, "I know you're angry. I know you're hurt. I understand. But I—"

"Cut the child psych, okay?"

She shook her head, her eyes stinging. "That's really mean. And unfair."

"Go below, Jody." He turned away, holding the wheel so tightly his knuckles gleamed white beneath his tanned skin. "Please. Go below. I'll have us there shortly."

"No, I won't go below. I want to work this out—"

Ignoring her, he reached down and pulled on the throttle, bringing the boat back up to speed.

Exhausted, Jody picked up her clothes and went below.

"This was not supposed to happen," she whispered into her hands as she lay curled on the bunk. "Am I wrong? What should I do?"

But her head was pounding. The migraine came marching back, beating its drums in her temples. She lay huddled into herself, and before she could find an answer, she faded off into a troubled sleep.

When she woke, everything was quiet.

"Eric?" she called, but there was no answer.

She climbed the ladder and found herself looking at a totally unfamiliar landscape: a metal dock, some small boats, a little rickety waterside restaurant: bar and gas station in one. Two men sat on the porch drinking beer, empty bottles lined up neatly along the railing in front of them. There was no one else around.

"Eric?" she called out, then bit her lip, realizing her error. "Eric?" she whispered.

She climbed onto the dock. "Excuse me," she

called. "Any chance you saw the man who brought in this boat?"

The thinner man jerked his head in the direction of the restaurant. "He went in there."

"Thanks." She nodded, hurrying past them.

Eric, in mustache and sunglasses and an old hooded sweatshirt, was sitting at the bar, watching her approach.

She closed the door quietly behind her and slid on to the next stool. "Hi."

"Hi," he answered, tipping the bottle up and taking a long pull on his beer.

"Are you okay?"

"Fine."

She nodded, not trusting her voice. Then she shrugged and tried a little smile. "So . . . are you gonna buy me a beer?"

"No time." The muscles along his jaw clenched and knotted. He took a breath, held it, then said, "Your cab's here. He'll take you back to Orlando."

"No!" she begged, the tears gathering on her lower lids.

"Go ahead, Jody, it'll be easier this way. Go do what you've gotta do. And in the meantime we'll work on it."

She shook her head, the ugly bar sparkling in the film of tears. When she blinked, they ran down her cheeks.

"I've paid the cab. And here's a few bucks just to buy some milk and cookies. Please, just take it. I'm in no mood to argue."

"Okay, okay."

"Okay."

"And I'll write. I will. I'll address my letters to Lena, *here*. Where *is* this, where are we?"

"Send it to Everglades City. Box Twenty-one. She'll pick it up."

"And we'll figure out what to do next, how to do it together. Right?"

"Right."

"You mean that, don't you, Eric?" she whispered, blinking back hot tears.

"Yes." He nodded, jaw clenched, eyes hidden beneath dark brows.

She waited a minute, then, reached out and touched his arm. "Don't I get a kiss?" she asked softly.

"Come back for it," he said.

Twelve

"Jody, aren't you there yet?! Shoot. Well, it's me, Anne. Again. For the umpteenth time. I wanna say thanks a lot, buddy. Not a call, not a note. Just left me here holding the bag. Well, to top it off, Steve's mom took sick, and we have to fly to Philadelphia, so the mutt's in the kennel over at Two Oaks. You can pick him up and baby-sit for me if you're so inclined, or just leave him there and I'll take out a second mortgage when I get back. In the meantime, the ceiling in—"

The message machine clicked off. Whirred. Continued.

"It's still me. Damn that machine! Anyway, the ceiling in room six has a leak. Fix it. I finished the painting, the cleaning, stocking the art closet *and* the supply cabinet. I placed the order with Constructive Playthings, but the prices went up, so I had to scratch some of the manipulatives. The order's on the desk. Check—"

Click. Whir. Anne's voice:

"Me! Check the other orders and do what you want . . . or what we can afford. Damn! Oh, the keys are in your dresser drawer, under your bras. I'll call from Philadelphia . . . not like some people I know. If I sound pissed, I am . . . but it's not all your fault . . . just most of it . . . well, hope you at least had fun.
I'll—"

Click. There were no further messages.

Thirteen

Three weeks passed. School reopened.

Like a fever, the need to tell someone about Eric burned within Jody. Here she was, in love with the most wonderful, most desirable, most gorgeous man in the world, and she was pledged to secrecy. Couldn't even tell her partner, her best friend, Anne.

Anne certainly asked: begged, bribed, cajoled, pleaded. *What* in heaven's name had happened on that mystery vacation of hers? Tell just a bit, a word . . . a single hint!

And Jody yearned to, yearned to mention the way Eric threw back his head when he laughed, the way his dark eyes shone, the way that smile of his cut right to the heart of her. It was better than a movie!

She wanted to whisper to someone that she

knew the man behind the mask, the real Eric Ransom . . . the man of flesh and blood, of passion and promises; that he and she made love in the ocean, in sunlight and moonlight; that she loved him more than she could possibly say!

Instead, she unplugged stuffed toilets, soothed tears, reprimanded biters, nursed baby dolls back to immediate health. She built block towers, finger-painted, led a parade of three-year-olds outside to feed the birds.

Birds!

Was there no one she could tell about the wonderful, breathtaking man who showed her where the great white herons nested?

Another week, and another.

Longer than the time she had spent with Eric. Yet he dominated her thoughts, her feelings, waking and sleeping, in a way that reality couldn't.

In a daze, it seemed, she moved through the early days of the school year, through parents' open house, the ordinary crisis of a teacher breaking her contract without notice and the hiring of a replacement. A three-year-old climbed up on the shelves in room 5, and the whole thing fell to the floor, child and all. Fortunately, only the wall was hurt. A mouse hole was discovered in the kitchen; Jody rescued three gray mice from the cracker cabinet, repaired the hole, and recleaned the entire kitchen. All of it passed in a haze.

But alone in her house each and every night, she'd sit down and write Eric letters, talking to him as if he were there across the kitchen table from her. She mailed them to the post-office box in Everglades City. And waited for an answer.

At night the letter was waiting on his desk.

Eric found it there when he came back from fishing. He'd stayed out too long, and his arms and shoulders were burned, stinging from salt and exposure. The pain felt good. It was something to think about. And the tiredness was good. Maybe tonight, finally, he'd sleep.

But there was the letter. Sometimes they came one at a time, and sometimes in clusters, like stars appearing against a black and empty sky.

He was never ready for them. Always felt ambushed, caught off guard, his defenses down. She did that to him. Stripped him of the protection he'd used for years, the shield he'd hammered out of anger, cynicism, and loneliness.

So they hurt.

Tonight, he gave the desk a wide berth and headed for the shower. He stood under the hot water, lathered, scrubbed, rinsed . . . toweled himself dry. In front of the mirror he kept his eyes averted, his back turned. He knew, without looking, that there would be hunger in his eyes, need, desire, pain . . . and he was tired of it! He wished he could run away, far away. He wished he could empty his mind, could control the ache that tore at his gut. He almost wished he'd never met her . . . but no! *that* would be worse. Sinking onto the edge of the bed, his dark head in his hands, he shut his eyes. No . . . he couldn't wish that; that would be truly unbearable.

This was merely hell!

Oh, Jody . . . Jody . . .

Stubbornly, he left the letter lying untouched and stomped off to dinner.

Meals were impossible now. Lena and Matthew had given up and agreed to eat alone, leaving him to his own bad company. He sat there in the dark, jaw clenched, muttering swearwords into his plate. He took a glass of cognac back to the bedroom with him afterward, and locked the door.

Had some kind spirit whisked the letter away, left his desk empty? Could the liquor erase the pictures that haunted his mind? No such luck.

Jody.

Picking up the envelope, he held it for a moment unopened, seeing her face there in the darkness, hearing the sound of her voice, feeling her touch. Her hands had held this paper, her fingertips, her gentle touch. He could feel it now, a soft caress on his brow, a touch on his cheek. He tipped his head as if to seek its warmth, but there was nothing there. Emptiness. Loss.

Should he go back? Could he? Was he just being stubborn? Maybe it wasn't as bad as he remembered it. Maybe he could survive this time. . . .

Opening the letter, his gaze leapt eagerly from

Dearest Eric to *All my love, Jody.* Then slowly, savoring every word, he reread it again and again until he had it memorized.

Dearest Eric,

I miss you so desperately. The days are still hot and humid, the children cranky by afternoon, and then, to top it all off, we had a fire drill yesterday during nap time! Unbelievable.

I was glad to get home and raced right to the mailbox. But, Eric . . . you still haven't written. Please . . . please, dearest, write to me. Talk to me. The silence is unbearable. . . .

He crumpled the sheet, tossed it into the corner and sat with his arms locked over his chest, glaring out to where sea would meet sky if only his eyes could see that far. If only wishes came true. If only magic were real! If only there were a happy-ever-after!

Damn.

Pushing open the French doors, he strode across the patio and down to the beach, running now, running hard, panting and out of breath by the time he reached the mangroves.

"Jody!" he shouted. "Jody, come back! Come back to me!"

Only the murmur of water among roots answered, that and the long, drawn-out cry of a heron.

• • •

On October 1 Jody invited Anne and Steve over for a Sunday afternoon picnic with the children. Amid the noise and chaos, she took Anne aside.

"Anne," she said, avoiding her friend's eyes, "I've got to talk to you. About the school."

"What now?" Anne groaned. "Don't tell me there's one more thing wrong with the plumbing, or I'm going to scream."

"No, it's not anything like that."

"Lucky thing, 'cause I've had it. I feel like every ounce of my strength goes into the school right now. I'm worn out."

Jody wanted to crawl under the lawn furniture and hide. But panic was gnawing at her stomach: the ache of missing Eric, the fear of losing him. She frowned, kicking at the grass with the toe of her sneaker. "Anne . . . I . . . I need to make a change."

Anne stopped fiddling with the handful of grapes she was holding. "What does that mean?"

"I can't say exactly. I just need to be free to make a sudden change if I should have to. I need . . ." She shook her head and tried again. "I want to sell—"

"Don't say it, Jo!"

"Anne, I want to sell my part of the business. To you. To someone else. Whatever I can manage quickly."

"You can't!" Anne shouted. "You just can't do that, Jody. Do you hear me?"

"Hey, what's going on here, you two?" Steve broke in, laughing. "Need a ref?"

"Jody's selling the business. 'Her part' as she calls it. Dammit, Jo, your part, my part—the whole thing runs together. Who's gonna love it the way you do? Who'd put up with all the crap? And you know I haven't got two extra cents to my name. Oh, Jody, you can't do this to me."

Jody felt awful, like the betrayer and betrayed both at the same time. "Oh, Anne, please, listen to me: This is the most important thing that's ever happened in my life. I'm in love, and I have to make it work."

"Oh, what is it? That vacation mystery man? I haven't heard one specific word about him, seen one glimpse of him . . . not even a picture. Who is he? *What* is he? *Why* won't you tell me?"

"I can't, I just can't—"

"Forget it. Do what you want. Kids," she yelled, tossing the grapes on the grass, "get your stuff together! We're going home."

"But, Mom, we didn't even eat!"

"Don't argue with me. Don't anyone dare say anything to me."

They left without a word of good-bye to Jody.

That night she went to the video store and rented three of Eric's movies. Holding a TV dinner on her lap, a glass of wine on the coffee table at her knee, she hit "play."

And there he was. Tall, broad-shouldered, his

dark hair shorter, but the same thick mane she had clutched with her hands. Watching him, she could feel the same shock travel up her arms. Her nipples ached.

He moved slowly, languidly, across the twenty-inch screen. He was so beautiful. And in person even more sensual than he appeared on the screen. She remembered the smell of his skin, the taste of his mouth. How the water had run in beads down his golden chest, the drops sliding into the curly dark hair until she wiped them away with her fingers.

She sat on her hands and bent forward, watching him, listening to his voice. She took his voice into her head, closed her eyes, and conjured him into the room: It was *her* he was speaking to. For her, the words of love, of desire.

But there on the screen he was holding someone else—what *was* her name?—someone slim and blond and elegant. It wasn't real. No, reality was a huge hole that had opened up between them, a chasm as wide as the Grand Canyon, Eric on one side, she on the other . . . and only love to bridge the empty space between.

Eric. Eric. Her tears ran off her chin, onto her lap. She cried without making a noise.

After what seemed like hours, she pushed the "eject" button and watched the video slide from its slot. She drove back to the store and dropped all three tapes on the counter.

"Got a thing for Eric Ransom, huh?" quipped the store clerk. "He was something, wasn't he!"

Jody hurried out into the dark. Her face felt

hot when she touched it, her cheeks burning. She pressed her hands to her mouth.

Got a "thing" for Eric Ransom?

What *was* real? Was *anything* real?

The next week she got the flu. And from somewhere, in some fevered dream, the idea came to her.

She called the Workshop in Miami and asked for Chandler.

"No, I don't know his last name, but how many Chandlers are there?" she demanded. "Sorry, I'm not feeling well. Could you please just tell him that Jody called, Jody Conners . . . from the island . . . I'm sick and I have to talk to him. It's important. Please? Thanks."

She hung up and lay back on the pillow, one arm thrown over her eyes, and refused to think. It was done.

Fourteen

Five days later Jody drove home from work and found a rental car parked in her driveway.

At first she thought it was empty. But then she could see someone—a man—slouched down in the driver's seat, a baseball cap pulled low over his face.

Her heart stopped.

She pulled up behind him and cut the engine. Shaking, she fumbled with the door handle and finally got it open. She was afraid to step out. Afraid of what she'd find . . . or wouldn't find. It could be anybody, just anybody. Oh Lord!

It hurt to breathe.

Slowly, she approached the other car. The man didn't move. She could see only the back of his head, the faded blue cap, the damp sandy hair plastered to his neck.

Sandy, sun-streaked hair?

Tears sprang to her eyes. Her nose stung. Her breath came out in a shudder of disappointment.

She hurried to the car, leaned down, and propped both elbows on the door. "Yeah? Can I help—"

Eric lifted his sunglasses and turned to face her. "I thought you were sick."

Jody almost fell down. Holding on to the car door, she reached through the open window and touched his shoulder, his cheek. "Oh, Eric, it's you."

He sat at the kitchen table, and she stood behind him, her arms wrapped around him, her cheek pressed to his cheek. She needed to feel him, touch him, just lean there against him. She didn't need anything else, didn't want anything else.

Every time he tried to talk, she'd tip her face around and kiss the corner of his mouth. "Not yet . . . not yet," she whispered. "Please. Not yet!"

He sat still, elbows propped on the table, hands resting on her arms crossed tightly over his chest. He could feel the way she shook every few minutes, as if the fear, the despair he'd seen in her face hadn't quite left her yet. She trembled like a key deer, like a small, frightened animal. He bit his tongue and gave her time.

Eyes closed, she rubbed her cheek against his. He'd grown a shadow of a beard, and she rubbed her skin against it, taking its scratchiness as pleasure. She deserved this minute of ecstasy for all the hours and days of loneliness she'd suffered . . . and was about to suffer. There was no doubt he was angry with her! She'd seen it flashing in his dark eyes. He thought she'd tricked him, tempted him out of safety, that she'd brought him here under false pretenses.

"Jody—"

"Shhh . . . one minute more? Please? And then . . . come lie down with me. Come lie down with me and hold me." She spoke into his ear, her breath warm on his cheek. "Before we talk. Before anything else."

He closed his eyes. A spasm of pain crossed his face. "No. We need to talk."

"I don't *want* to talk," she pleaded.

"Then you can listen." Taking hold of one hand, he brought her around from behind him. He pushed a chair out for her, folded his arms, and waited for her to sit down.

She sat.

"Jody," he began, "you—"

"You think I lied to you. But I didn't. I *was* sick! And worse, my *heart* was sick. My heart was breaking, and I just couldn't stand it. I came back here thinking I knew what I was doing . . . that I was doing the right thing, the sensible thing . . . but without you, nothing made any sense. And you didn't answer my letters, didn't write me a note, send me a message, *nothing*, not one thing to say you loved me . . . that you really *did* love me . . . that there was a way to make it all work. How, *how*, could you *do* that to me? How could you not write back, call, something?"

"I was angry. You're the one who left, who walked out—"

"I had to!"

"So you said. But that didn't change how it felt. I was angry at you, and I wanted you to feel as bad as I felt. I wanted you to hurt too."

"But, Eric, that's so mean—"

"I felt mean!" he snapped, slamming one hand flat on the table hard enough to make the napkin holder jump. "I wanted you to miss me as much as I was missing you. I wanted you to give up, give in, cry uncle!"

"Then . . . you do love me?"

He looked at her then, pain washing across his face. He shook his head slowly in frustration. "Yes, I love you. I just can't love you here."

"Of course you can. Just give it a try. For me. For *us*." She sat in his lap and wrapped her arms around his neck. She pushed her hands through his hair and pressed her tongue into his mouth.

Between kisses his mouth brushed across her skin. His hands were all over her. His breath was coming in ragged gasps.

"Nothing bad can happen. You'll see, you'll see," she whispered. She slipped her hands under his shirt and pulled it off over his head. She undid his belt, unbuttoned his pants, slid her hands down over his body. Lifting her weight, she straddled him on the chair.

Surprised into a grin, he stared at her. Then

he stood, gave her a second to wrap her legs around his hips, and headed through the living room. "Which way's the bedroom?" he asked.

"Straight ahead. Second star on the right, and straight on till morning."

He laughed. "I thought that was Never-Never Land?"

"Oh, I love when I can make you laugh," she whispered, kissing his chin, his nose, his mouth, with small, tender kisses that promised more. "It's the best sound I've ever heard."

"Show me where the bedroom is, and we'll see what else I can come up with," he said softly, then followed where she pointed.

"You look so different with light hair," she said later, brushing it back from his forehead with the tips of her fingers.

"Different enough, I hope," he said. "Though I brought a matching mustache. And a pair of horn-rimmed glasses. Not taking any chances."

"Then you're going to stay?" she asked breathlessly, watching his face.

"We'll see. For a little while, I guess. You make it very hard to leave."

"My wish come true." She snuggled up close to him, covering his legs with her leg, draping an arm across his chest. "Oh, Eric, it'll be all right. You'll see. You'll be glad you're here."

He sighed. "At this moment I'm glad I'm here, I have to admit that much. I missed you, the feel of you, the fun of you." He hugged her close.

It made her weep.

"Oh, no . . . not again."

"I can't help it. I'm just so happy, so happy. . . ."

"Lena and Matthew were not thrilled with this plan."

"And Chandler?"

Eric gave a snort. "Chandler was furious."

"I'll bet there are more descriptive words to describe Chandler's reaction—"

"—and he used them all! He used words that even made *me* cringe!"

"Not a happy camper."

"Not a happy *friend*," Eric corrected softly. "He really did not think this was a good idea."

"And Lena agreed? Matthew too?"

" 'Fraid so. They've seen me after a bout with the television cameras, a losing round with hysterical fans."

"But there's none of that here. There's only me."

"If we don't go out. If we hide," he said softly. Ominously.

Going off to work the next morning was torture, and she hurried home the minute the last car-pool mom turned out of the parking lot.

She found Eric pacing the living-room floor. The newspaper was strewn all over the couch, the radio hummed in the kitchen, even the TV was on, the volume turned off, nameless, soundless figures floating across the screen.

"Are you okay?" She laughed nervously, as if confronting an eccentric relative.

"I'm going crazy. I feel caged."

"Then let's go out. Put on your mustache and your baseball cap and your glasses, and give it a shot." She flashed her most winning smile. "Come on. Nothing bad will happen." She hoped.

It felt the way a nightmare did.

Things that happened seemed unstoppable. One thing led to another. There was no hiding, no escape, as if no matter how fast they ran, the footsteps behind them closed the distance. No matter how hard they tried, the doors wouldn't open, the exit was blocked. One look, one whisper, one hand reaching out . . . and suddenly there were crowds: Strangers gathered, pressing close, reaching, touching, grabbing. And through it all they were silent, the scream stuck in their throats.

"Did anyone ever tell you, you look a lot like that movie star Eric Ransom?" The girl handing him the ice-cream cone giggled, blushing, but she held the cone aloft so Eric had to reach over the counter to get it, touching her hand as he did. She batted her lashes at him, laughing, shouting to her co-worker, "Hey, Cindy, doesn't this guy look just like Eric Ransom?"

"What do I owe you?"

"Two double scoops on waffle cones . . . let's see—" Hip cocked, lips pursed, she kept flirting right in front of Jody, as if Jody didn't even exist.

"Here's a ten. Keep the change." Eric tossed the money on the counter and turned away.

"Hey, thanks! And come back soon. I mean it."

Jody hit the sidewalk fuming. "That flirt! That little—"

"It's not her fault, it's ours. There's an old saying: 'If you can't stand the heat, stay out of the kitchen.' "

"But that's ridiculous. You should be able to go where you want, do what you want—"

"But I can't. And *shoulds* don't matter. The fact is, I can't."

"I won't believe that."

"No? Fine. Have it your way."

He strode along, tossing his untasted cone into a trash can.

Heads turned. People stared or did double takes in passing.

Eric ignored them, walking along, baseball cap pulled down, hands stuffed in his pockets. At his side Jody noticed every sidelong glance, every stare. It appalled her. This wasn't possible. Surely, they couldn't all recognize him . . . and if they did, they'd have the courtesy not to gape and gawk like visitors at the zoo.

Finally, when her chocolate–chocolate-chip ice cream was dripping down her hand and off her wrist, she unlooped her arm from his and leaned back against a storefront. "Whoa. Sorry. I've got to stop for a second; I just can't lick and run at the same time."

His eyes seemed to refocus, seeing her for the first time in minutes. "Sure," he said softly. "Sorry." One corner of his mouth pulled down in a wry grin. "You're a mess."

"I know." She laughed, fumbling at her sticky hand with a wet and soggy napkin. "Wanna lick?"

He shook his head, the sun glinting off his sandy hair, his gorgeous smile. There were crinkle lines around his eyes again, and the frown was gone.

"What I want is a chance to take a boat out, or run hard across a field, do some work, do *something* to get rid of this damn tension—"

"Would sex help?"

He laughed. "Wouldn't hurt."

Jody's answering laugh became a gasp as someone pounded on the glass behind her head. She spun, expecting an angry face telling her to move on, but instead a group was gathered there, all eager eyes and open mouths. They were smiling, waving, beckoning, and pointing at Eric.

He backed toward the curb, turning, shading his face with one hand.

Before Jody could even move, someone had dashed out of the store. "It's you, isn't it?" she cried. "It is, I know it. The minute you smiled, I knew it. I said to my friends, 'Look, it's Eric Ransom!' "

"We *all* said so," cried another. "I knew it too.

I said, he's just got his hair lighter, like he did in *The Empty Doorway*. I told my wife—"

"What's going on? What's happening?"

"Who is it?"

"Is it him? Really?"

"Who? What's going on?"

"It's Eric Ransom! Really! Are you back for good? Are you going to make movies again?"

"Can I have your autograph? Oh, I think I'm going to faint."

"What's going on? Who? Is it really him? Is that his girlfriend?"

"Mr. Ransom, could you just sign my hand? Please?"

They got back to Jody's house in one piece . . . basically. The baseball cap was gone, snatched off Eric's head. There was a lipstick smudge at the corner of his mouth, a dark red stain like a bruise.

Jody sank into a chair, exhausted, stunned. "I don't believe this."

"You keep saying that." He sounded disgusted, glaring down at her, his eyes hard. "How much proof do you want?"

"I don't want *any*! I just want them all to go away! I want people to stop it, stop acting like that, stop taking such liberties, stop being so . . . so horrible, so grabbing! I want—"

"It doesn't matter what you want. Or what I want. It's just the way it is."

"But it's wrong. Unfair."

He snorted and turned away. "Who said there's anything fair in this world?"

She leapt to her feet, anger giving her strength. She grabbed his shoulder, then spun him around. "I won't accept that. And you shouldn't either. You've got to fight back!"

He groaned, pushing his fingers through his hair. "What do you think I did all those years in Hollywood? What the hell do you think I've been doing these five damn years on the island. I *am* fighting back! In the only way there is. Just because you think there's some magic answer to all our problems doesn't make it so."

"Then what do we do? *You* tell *me*."

"I've gotten by, haven't I?"

"No!" She shook her head, chin up, eyes flashing. "That's not enough. 'Getting by' is just not good enough. Not for *you*. Not for *us*." Her voice dropped to a whisper. "Eric, I believe you were just waiting for me on that island. I really believe that . . . that you were just waiting for me to find you—"

"Oh God, Jody, you're wearing me out with all these damn fairy tales. They're only make-believe. No . . . if you love me, you are just going to have to accept the limitations of my life."

"What? And hide away on that island hidden by mangroves, lost in the Everglades? Is that what you want? Is that the life you want? Or is that *just* surviving? And on *their* terms! Oh, Eric," she pleaded, taking his face in her hands. "Let's keep trying. We'll figure it out together—"

He stepped back, away from her touch. "Call and make a dinner reservation. Somewhere elegant. Extravagant. Use your name. Then watch what happens."

At nine that night they gave the car to the valet and rode the elevator up to the twenty-seventh floor. Below them, Disney World, Epcot, Universal Studios . . . all of Orlando was spread like a cluster of jewels heaped on black velvet.

The maître d' approached, solemn, aloof. "Good evening. Do you have a . . ." He stumbled, hesitated. His eyes widened. "Do you have a reservation, sir? Mr. Ransom? It *is* Mr. Ransom, isn't it?"

"The reservation is under my friend's name: Conners."

"Oh yes, sir, yes, of course. I understand. But if you had let us know, I would have reserved you the finest table—"

"I'm sure that whatever you've reserved for us is fine."

"Yes, yes, of course." Stumbling over his words, his feet, the maître d' backed his way across the room as if he were afraid that if he took his eyes off Eric, Eric would disappear. "This way, please."

Eric held Jody's elbow in a merciless grip.

"You know, now that the studios have opened here in Orlando, we get lots of celebrities joining us for dinner. But I had no idea . . . I mean, I didn't know that you . . . that you were out of hid . . . that you were back in the public eye."

"I'm not. I'm just here for dinner with a friend."

"Of course, *of course*! Mum's the word!" With a wink he scooted Jody's chair in, ready or not, and disappeared into the kitchen.

Eyes were watching from other tables. Conversation ceased. The whole room was silent, waiting.

Eric unfolded his napkin and dropped it in his lap. He looked across the table at Jody and lifted one dark brow.

Jody gave the slightest of shrugs. The silence was oppressive, eerie. She was afraid to move, afraid to swallow. Looking down at the tablecloth in front of her, she thought, *This is awful. I hate this.*

As if he read her mind, Eric reached across the table for her hand.

She took it, weaving her fingers through his in gratitude, in happiness, the tears starting to her eyes. She smiled at him. "I don't know whether to be bold and courageous or go hide under the table," she admitted in a whisper, laughing, leaning toward him, toward the safety of his broad shoulders and dark eyes. . . .

And that was just how the flash caught them, froze them, blinding them for an instant.

"Oh, I was sure you wouldn't mind. I just couldn't believe it. Here we are on our first night in Orlando, and who do we see but Eric Ransom! The folks back home in Houston will just go wild."

"Give me that film."

"What?" the woman asked, the camera still half-raised in front of her.

"I said, *give me that film.*" Eric's voice was harsh, restrained, but his anger made the muscles pop along his clenched jaw. "Did you hear me?"

"I will not!" the woman yelled, clutching the camera to her chest. "It's my camera, and this is a free country! Who do you think you are, anyway?"

"Who do *I*—"

Jody caught Eric's arm as he rose from the table, and she held on tight, pulling him back down. "Eric, forget it. It's okay. Come on, it's not worth—"

Eric was on his feet now, and Jody could see how furious he was, how close to completely losing control. He looked dangerous suddenly, wild and unpredictable, frightening.

"Eric," she whispered, squeezing his hand. His fingers felt like ice in hers, ice-cold, unresponsive. "Eric . . ."

"Let's go." That frozen grip pulled her to her feet. She hurried after him, voices chasing them, words flung at their backs.

"Who the hell does he think he is, anyway!"

"Stuck-up son of a bitch."

He stopped the car in front of Jody's house. Keeping both hands on the wheel, he spoke into the darkness. "I'm going. Are you coming with me?"

"Eric . . . I—"

He leaned across her, his shoulder roughly brushing her breasts, and snapped open her door. "Coming with me? Or staying?"

"I love you. I want to be with you forever. But I won't run away. That's not the answer."

"It's the only one I have. Take it or leave it."

"Stop it! Ultimatums and anger, that's not for us. Eric, please. Come in and let me love you, let me comfort you—"

"I don't want to be comforted. Hell, I need my anger; it keeps me going."

"Eric, please, calm down and listen to me for a minute—"

"Not one minute more, not one second." His dark eyes burned with pain, but his jaw was set. "Maybe I *do* want you to throw this all away. Maybe I *do* need you to say you'd hide away in the swamp with me. Maybe I do need you to lose everything, give up everything, to have *me*. Maybe that is exactly what I need, sensible or not. Selfish or not. Maybe I need to know that *nothing* I'd ask would be too much." He glared at her, eyes narrowed in fury. "Or, Jody, if the hope of glamour is gone . . . do you not want me anymore?"

She grabbed his shoulders, her hands crumpling the smooth fabric of his jacket, the crisp white shirt beneath. She wanted to get to his skin, dig into his flesh, wake something in those cold dark eyes. "Eric, I want you more than ever. Because it's you I love—the man, not the myth. You! But this isn't the way to prove it—"

He pushed her hands away and shifted into drive.

Jody swiped at her tears with the back of her hand. "Eric, please, listen to me—"

The car started to move.

She jumped out, saw him grab wildly at the door handle, miss, and then pull it shut, as the car roared away from the curb.

She couldn't believe it. She stood there, waiting for him to come back. In a minute, one minute more, he'd be back, she told herself. He'd circle the block and reappear, right there in front of her. In a minute. One more minute. He'd be back, his anger cooled. Around the block, or down to the first traffic light. Any minute now . . .

And then she started to run. Feet pounding, heart pounding, she ran down the street in the dark, running after him, running for her life. But there was only the hollow echo of her feet and her cries in the night.

He was gone.

Fifteen

Jody didn't see or hear from Eric for a month. Thirty-one days. Seven hundred forty-four hours. Forty-four thousand, six-hundred forty seconds. She counted every one.

In that time she borrowed money from her parents, who had to borrow it from the bank. But she did it, sensible or not. She bought out Anne, who was exceedingly grateful, then sold the preschool on the first offer she got. She sold her house at a loss, definitely not sensible, but done. Finished. Then she paid back her parents, who shook their heads but kept their own counsel—thank heavens!—just gave her hugs and helped her move into an apartment.

Finally, she made two purchases. One was a dog, a little Shetland sheepdog puppy. "A dog?" her parents groaned as they watched her lay newspapers on the kitchen floor. The other was a secret. Then she sent a letter to the post-office box in Everglades City and another inside an envelope addressed to Chandler in Miami.

But Eric could have been anywhere by then: Europe, South America, the moon.

At night she'd look up at the moon, shining there so calm and cool, untroubled. She'd wish on the first star . . . the second, on every star that appeared.

But nothing happened.

And then one afternoon an envelope arrived. Inside was an invitation—formal, elegant, printed on embossed stationery—to a cocktail party up in Heathrow, a neighborhood she'd never been to and never expected to be: ritzy, elite, a little enclave carved out by money with its own post office and exit from the interstate. The opposite end of the city, and a place where she didn't know a soul.

There was a date, a time—that was all. Not even an RSVP; obviously regrets were not accepted.

Puzzled, excited, not being one bit sensible, Jody went out and bought a pretty dress, a little black thing that only came to the middle of her thighs. She also bought a sexy nightgown and folded it in tissue and laid it on top of her suitcase, the suitcase already packed and waiting at the foot of her bed. She put it in the trunk of her car. She put the puppy in the backseat, her surprise in the glove compartment, and drove the forty-five minutes north.

The house was enormous, a palace. Every light was on in the windows, like a beacon in the darkness. Jody parked up close on the circular drive, gave the puppy a milkbone, left the windows open a crack, and locked the car.

Her hands were trembling. Her palms were wet. She reopened the car door and wiped her hands on the velour seat, then locked the car again. Her heart was pounding like a drum.

A butler led her through the foyer into the living room. There were sixteen or maybe twenty people there, sipping drinks, eating canapés. Her host, a man she recognized from articles in the newspaper and a local magazine, introduced her to everyone, settled her comfortably with a group on one sofa, and brought her a glass of white wine. Everyone was courteous, friendly. The conversation centered around the opening of the new art museum, and it was pleasant, charming. Jody hadn't the vaguest idea what she was doing there.

She looked up at every movement, started at every sound, peered into every corner. But everything seemed to be exactly what it was . . . and none of it made any sense.

When she tried to talk to the host, he slipped away; there was someone he *had* to speak to for a moment. Could he perhaps get her another glass of wine?

Another glass of wine on top of these nerves and I'll faint dead away, Jody thought. She rolled her eyes heavenward, pressed a hand to her throat, set her glass down on the coffee table with a clunk.

"Another glass of wine, Ms. Conners?"

"Oh no, no thank you, I'm fine, thank you so much."

And then a few good nights. One couple left, and then a group of three. Now there were just a few of them rattling around in this big house, smiling, chatting. . . .

Should I leave? Could he be waiting outside? Should I try to look into the other rooms? What am I supposed to do?

Or was this all some kind of a ghastly mistake? Was this all exactly as it seemed to be, and she'd somehow received an invitation by mistake, a name erroneously picked from the museum membership list, and her host as puzzled as she was? Oh heaven help me, she prayed silently. Let there be some other reason . . . some crazy, wonderful reason. And please, let Eric be here.

There. She'd said it. The wish . . . the one and only wish that meant anything: *Let Eric be here.*

Star light, star bright, first star I see tonight . . .

"Some more wine, Ms. Conners?"

"No thank you. But sit down, please. Tell me—"

"What?"

She looked at him, tears brimming at her lower lids, her chin raised, shoulders squared. "Is there . . . is there something you're supposed to tell me? Something I'm supposed to do?"

"I really don't know, my dear. I was asked to include you this evening, which was my pleasure, and then at ten I'm to show a film in the screening room."

"At ten?" she repeated. "Well, what time is it? Do you have a watch, does anyone have a watch?"

"It's nine-fifteen."

"Nine-fifteen!" She dug her fingers into his arm. "Show the film."

"But I was asked—"

"Show the film now, this instant, this second, or I am going to stand on the top of this coffee table and scream!" She put one foot up on the beveled glass, but he grabbed her.

"Okay, okay! Come with me."

In the darkened room the projector hummed. One beam of light, diffused, catching dust motes in its path, turned the pull-down screen to white. Numbers flashed: nine, eight, seven, six, an upside-down four, three . . . all the hallmarks of a home movie. Two . . . one . . . the screen gone blank for an instant, and then the scene took focus:

A gorgeous man alone on a beach at sunset. He's unshaven, rumpled, barefoot. He stands there, back to the camera, musing and soliloquizing, his voice directed at the impassive ocean, the unfeeling mangroves . . . speaking aloud of his life, his angers and fears, his hopes and desires. Until, as the sun dropped like a golden coin into the blue pocket of the sea, he turned and faced the camera.

Eric.

There he was, the actor, the *man* . . . Eric Ransom . . . facing the camera and looking every bit as bold and heroic as he always did on the silver screen, yet strangely vulnerable too.

Eric, looking out at his unseen audience, saying softly, "I want a life with meaning and joy. Hard work done well. A home. Children. A dog. Happiness: a hand to hold across the breakfast table, and a cup of tea late at night in front of the fire, with someone's head resting on my shoulder. No more running away. No more hiding, no more living in anger and isolation. I want to be done with all that. Someone told me it's not enough . . . not enough to settle for. She was right. It just took me a while to really hear her, believe her.

"Now the question is, can she hear me? Will she believe me when I tell her that I know of a place, a bonny place with broad fields bounded by the wild sea, villages filled with neighbors, and friends, thatch-roofed cottages with smoke curling from their chimneys, with sheep at play in the meadows and children racing across the hills. Will she hear me? Will she believe me? Will she go with me?

"I can see it in my mind's eye, waiting. I can feel the wind against my face, the sun on my head, her hand in mine. I can imagine it all."

He paused, licked dry lips, continued. "But is it just a dream? Or can we make this fairy tale come true?"

There was silence in the room. Then total darkness. Then a voice, well known and loved, in Jody's ear. "Well? What do you say, love?"

She turned and faced him, fighting back tears, the words spilling from her lips. "I say that I love you, more than I ever dreamed or wished or hoped to love a man. I love you so much that I would have gone to live in that swamp with you, come hurricane, hell, or high water. I would have hidden there with nothing but you, and it would have been enough. Because without you, there is nothing. But with you, everything is possible.

"So I say yes . . . a thousand—a million—times yes . . . to this future you dream. We'll make it real together. Forever. Yes, yes, my love, my dearest, yes. . . . and if you don't kiss me this minute, I'm going to die!"

So he kissed her. Took her in his arms, bent his head to hers, and kissed her outrageously.

Only the fleeting thought that her host might be somewhere about kept Jody from pulling Eric down on the couch. As it was, she ran her hands hungrily over his hair, his neck, his shoulders, his back. "Oh . . . I have missed you, missed you," she repeated, kissing him again and again. "Never, ever, again am I going to let you out of my sight."

"Never," he agreed, smiling that heart-stopping smile of his, his dark eyes shining with happiness.

"Oh my goodness," she exclaimed, joy spilling out of her in a gush of laughter. "Have *I* got some surprises for *you*: two tickets, first class, to Scotland. And your sheepdog's in the car. I named her Lassie. Not very original, but it was that or Rumpelstiltskin!"

Eric laughed as she knew he would. As she hoped he would. As she had dreamed he would. "How in the world did you know?"

"Because I do." She grinned. "Because I always will. Because it was meant to be."

There was a discreet tapping at the door.

When Eric disentangled himself from Jody's arms, he found the butler waiting outside, holding a tray with a bottle of champagne and two crystal glasses.

"It was thought that a toast might be in order." Solemnly, he pulled the door closed behind him.

Eric popped the cork and poured champagne into both glasses. Giving one to Jody, he entwined his hand with hers till his glass was at her lips, and hers at his. "A toast, my love: to happy ever after."

They drank.

And, as in all good fairy tales, that wish was destined to come true.

Epilogue

"You're late!" Jody cried, pulling open the door the instant she heard Eric's approaching steps.

"No, I'm not," he said, hugging her to him. "It's just a wee bit after five."

He was wearing trousers, wool socks and boots, a white wool sweater, and an open jacket. His cap was in his hand, and his hair was windblown. His eyes were shining, and he was smiling, an excited grin that stretched from ear to ear. "Come out with me a minute. There's something I want you to hear!"

Jody grabbed the sweater hanging on the hook behind the door, and they dashed out together, into sunlight and wind. The morning had been filled with showers, and even now the smell of rain rose from the clean Scottish grass and the woolly backs of the sheep. But that was not what Eric wanted to show her.

"Listen!" he said, and then she heard it. From somewhere up on the hillside behind her, a bird was singing, a sound so unexpected, so familiar, it made her burst out laughing: *Cuckoo . . . Cuckoo . . .*

"Isn't that wild?" Eric laughed. At first I thought someone from the next croft—John or Andrew or someone—was playing a joke on me. But it's the real thing!"

"Can we climb and see it?" Jody asked, already racing up through the heather.

Eric caught up to her, and they climbed together. "Take it easy," he warned, slipping a hand around her waist. "Watch your step here. Careful of that branch—"

"Stop worrying!" she admonished, even as she shook her head and rolled her eyes. "This baby is going to climb hills like a little mountain goat! Relax!"

"Relax, she says, then goes leaping up mountainsides when she's six months pregnant," he grumbled, but his grin widened. "Here. This way . . . Look!"

In a wild stand of rhododendron perched the cuckoo, singing its head off.

Jody and Eric sat side by side on a rock, listening, looking out at the plowed fields, the meadows and grassy hillsides, the village rooftops, the cottages and barns dotting the scattered crofts, the distant edge of the sea. . . . all the things and places that were now home.

She rested her head on his shoulder. "We'd better get back," she finally said with a sigh.

"I've a pie to finish. We're invited to Lena and Matthew's for dinner: She's come up with some wonderful new recipe for mutton stew, something with sage and thyme and wild raspberries, I think. And Matthew is spinning wool and weaving. He's promised to teach me and make me a loom as soon as he's done with the cradle for our wee bonny babe." She folded her hands contentedly on her stomach, but, as usual, quiet lasted only a moment. "Look! There's Margaret, out taking Caroline for a walk. Hi, Margaret!" she called, waving her arms above her head. "Up here!"

In a minute they were running downhill calling.

"It's a wonderful day, right enough," the woman greeted them. "I was just on my way over to yours to ask you to a party tonight. At the pub. We're celebrating Donald's promotion. Just came in the mail this afternoon. Will you come?"

"Oh, we'd love to . . . but we're having dinner with Lena and Matthew—"

"Good! Save me having to trundle my invitation way over there. And tell Matthew he's to bring his banjo, and we'll have us some dancing. Eight o'clock then. 'Bye-bye just now."

"'Bye-bye!"

Walking back toward home, they heard what seemed to be an echo. *Bah . . . bah. Bah bah . . .*

It was a lamb, stuck in a thornbush.

Eric swung it up over his shoulders and carried it down to the fold, the animal bleating and crying and making a whole to-do all the while.

Lassie raced out and gathered in the little one, herding it back to its mother. Eric took just a moment to watch the reunion, then strolled back to Jody. When she rubbed her face against his, she smelled the woolly scent of sheep.

"ummmm . . ." she teased, "is that Obsession? Tuscany? Or is it perhaps Giorgio?"

"Eau de ewe!" Laughter rumbled in his chest and carried clear across the field. He threw back his head, smiling at the heavens, happy, truly happy.

Watching him, Jody smiled also. His laughter was the sound she loved best above all others in the world. For her, it was the sound of happy ever after.

THE EDITOR'S CORNER

Come join the celebration next month when LOVE-SWEPT reaches its tenth anniversary! When the line was started, we made a very important change in the way romance was being published. At the time, most romance authors published under a pseudonym, but we were so proud of our authors that we wanted to give them the credit and personal recognition they deserved. Since then LOVESWEPT authors have always written under their own names and their pictures appear on the inside covers of the books.

Right from the beginning LOVESWEPT was at the cutting edge, and as our readership changes, we change with them. In the process, we have nurtured writing stars, not only for romance, but for the publishing industry as a whole. We're proud of LOVESWEPT and the authors whose words we have brought to countless readers over the last ten years.

The lineup next month is indeed something to be proud about, with romances from five authors who have been steady—and stellar—contributors to LOVESWEPT since the very beginning and one up-and-coming name. Further, each of these six books carries a special anniversary message from the author to you. So don't let the good times pass you by. Pick up all six books, then sit back and enjoy!

The first of these treasures is **WILDFIRE**, LOVE-SWEPT #618 by Billie Green. Nobody can set aflame a woman's passion like Tanner West. He's spent his life breaking the rules—and more than a few hearts—and makes being bad seem awfully good. Though small-town Texas lawyer Rae Anderson wants a man who'd care for her and give her children, she finds herself rising to Tanner's challenge to walk on the wild side. This breathtaking romance is just what you've come to expect from super-talented Billie!

Kay Hooper continues her *Men of Mysteries Past* series with **THE TROUBLE WITH JARED**, LOVESWEPT #619. Years before, Jared Chavalier had been obsessed by Danica Gray, but her career as a gemologist had driven them apart. Now she arrives in San Francisco to work on the Mysteries Past exhibit of jewelry and discovers Jared there. And with a dangerous thief afoot, Jared must risk all to protect the only woman he's ever loved. Kay pulls out all the stops with this utterly stunning love story.

WHAT EMILY WANTS, LOVESWEPT #620 by Fayrene Preston, shocks even Emily Stanton herself, but she accepts Jay Barrett's bargain—ten days of her company for the money she so desperately needs. The arrangement is supposed to be platonic, but Emily soon finds she'll do just about anything . . . except let herself fall in love with the man whose probing questions drive her into hiding the truth. Fayrene delivers an intensely emotional and riveting read with this different kind of romance.

'TIL WE MEET AGAIN, LOVESWEPT #621 by Helen Mittermeyer, brings Cole Whitford and Fidelia Peters together at a high school reunion years after she'd disappeared from his life. She's never told him the heartbreaking reason she'd left town, and once the silken web of memories ensnares them both, they have to decide whether to let the past divide them once more . . . or to admit to a love that time has made only more precious. Shimmering with heartfelt emotion, **'TIL WE MEET AGAIN** is Helen at her finest.

Romantic adventure has never been as spellbinding as **STAR-SPANGLED BRIDE**, LOVESWEPT #622 by Iris Johansen. When news station mogul Gabe Falkner is taken by terrorists, he doesn't expect anyone to come to his rescue, least of all a golden-haired angel. But photojournalist Ronnie Dalton would dare anything to set free the man who'd saved her from death years ago, the one man she's always adored, the only man she dares not love. Iris works her bestselling magic with this highly sensual romance.

Last is **THE DOCTOR TAKES A WIFE**, LOVESWEPT #623 by Kimberli Wagner. The doctor is Connor MacLeod, a giant of a Scot who pours all his emotions into his work, but whose heart doesn't come alive until he meets jockey Alix Benton. For the first time since the night her life was nearly ruined, Alix doesn't fear a man's touch. Then suspicious accidents begin to happen, and Connor must face the greatest danger to become Alix's hero. Kimberli brings her special touch of humor and sizzling desire to this terrific romance.

On sale this month from Bantam are four spectacular women's fiction novels. From *New York Times* bestselling author Amanda Quick comes **DANGEROUS**, a breathtaking tale of an impetuous miss—and a passion that leads to peril. Boldness draws Prudence Merryweather into one dangerous episode after another, while the notorious Earl of Angelstone finds himself torn between a raging hunger to possess her and a driving need to keep her safe.

Patricia Potter's new novel, **RENEGADE**, proves that she is a master storyteller of historical romance. Set during the tumultuous days right after the Civil War, **RENEGADE** is the passionate tale of Rhys Redding, the Welsh adventurer who first appeared in **LIGHTNING** and Susannah Fallon, who must trust Rhys with her life while on a journey through the lawless South.

Pamela Simpson follows the success of **FORTUNE'S CHILD** with the contemporary novel **MIRROR, MIRROR**. When an unexpected inheritance entangles Alexandra Wyatt with a powerful family, Allie finds herself falling in love. And as she succumbs to Rafe Sloan's seductive power, she comes to suspect that he knows something of the murder she'd witnessed as a child.

In a dazzling debut, Geralyn Dawson delivers **THE TEXAN'S BRIDE**, the second book in Bantam's series of ONCE UPON A TIME romances. Katie Starr knows the rugged Texan is trouble the moment he steps into her father's inn, yet even as Branch is teasing his way into the lonely young widow's heart, Katie fears her secret would surely drive him away from her.

Also on sale this month in the Doubleday hardcover edition is **MOONLIGHT, MADNESS, AND MAGIC**, an anthology of original novellas by Suzanne Forster, Charlotte Hughes, and Olivia Rupprecht, in which a journal and a golden locket hold the secret to breaking an ancient family curse.

Happy reading!

With warmest wishes,

Nita Taublib

Nita Taublib
Associate Publisher

OFFICIAL RULES TO WINNERS CLASSIC SWEEPSTAKES

No Purchase necessary. To enter the sweepstakes follow instructions found elsewhere in this offer. You can also enter the sweepstakes by hand printing your name, address, city, state and zip code on a 3" x 5" piece of paper and mailing it to: Winners Classic Sweepstakes, P.O. Box 785, Gibbstown, NJ 08027. Mail each entry separately. Sweepstakes begins 12/1/91. Entries must be received by 6/1/93. Some presentations of this sweepstakes may feature a deadline for the Early Bird prize. If the offer you receive does, then to be eligible for the Early Bird prize your entry must be received according to the Early Bird date specified. Not responsible for lost, late, damaged, misdirected, illegible or postage due mail. Mechanically reproduced entries are not eligible. All entries become property of the sponsor and will not be returned.

Prize Selection/Validations: Winners will be selected in random drawings on or about 7/30/93, by VENTURA ASSOCIATES, INC., an independent judging organization whose decisions are final. Odds of winning are determined by total number of entries received. Circulation of this sweepstakes is estimated not to exceed 200 million. Entrants need not be present to win. All prizes are guaranteed to be awarded and delivered to winners. Winners will be notified by mail and may be required to complete an affidavit of eligibility and release of liability which must be returned within 14 days of date of notification or alternate winners will be selected. Any guest of a trip winner will also be required to execute a release of liability. Any prize notification letter or any prize returned to a participating sponsor, Bantam Doubleday Dell Publishing Group, Inc., its participating divisions or subsidiaries, or VENTURA ASSOCIATES, INC. as undeliverable will be awarded to an alternate winner. Prizes are not transferable. No multiple prize winners except as may be necessary due to unavailability, in which case a prize of equal or greater value will be awarded. Prizes will be awarded approximately 90 days after the drawing. All taxes, automobile license and registration fees, if applicable, are the sole responsibility of the winners. Entry constitutes permission (except where prohibited) to use winners' names and likenesses for publicity purposes without further or other compensation.

Participation: This sweepstakes is open to residents of the United States and Canada, except for the province of Quebec. This sweepstakes is sponsored by Bantam Doubleday Dell Publishing Group, Inc. (BDD), 666 Fifth Avenue, New York, NY 10103. Versions of this sweepstakes with different graphics will be offered in conjunction with various solicitations or promotions by different subsidiaries and divisions of BDD. Employees and their families of BDD, its division, subsidiaries, advertising agencies, and VENTURA ASSOCIATES, INC., are not eligible.

Canadian residents, in order to win, must first correctly answer a time limited arithmetical skill testing question. Void in Quebec and wherever prohibited or restricted by law. Subject to all federal, state, local and provincial laws and regulations.

Prizes: The following values for prizes are determined by the manufacturers' suggested retail prices or by what these items are currently known to be selling for at the time this offer was published. Approximate retail values include handling and delivery of prizes. Estimated maximum retail value of prizes: 1 Grand Prize ($27,500 if merchandise or $25,000 Cash); 1 First Prize ($3,000); 5 Second Prizes ($400 each); 35 Third Prizes ($100 each); 1,000 Fourth Prizes ($9.00 each) ; 1 Early Bird Prize ($5,000); Total approximate maximum retail value is $50,000. Winners will have the option of selecting any prize offered at level won. Automobile winner must have a valid driver's license at the time the car is awarded. Trips are subject to space and departure availability. Certain black-out dates may apply. Travel must be completed within one year from the time the prize is awarded. Minors must be accompanied by an adult. Prizes won by minors will be awarded in the name of parent or legal guardian.

For a list of Major Prize Winners (available after 7/30/93): send a self-addressed, stamped envelope entirely separate from your entry to: Winners Classic Sweepstakes Winners, P.O. Box 825, Gibbstown, NJ 08027. Requests must be received by 6/1/93. DO NOT SEND ANY OTHER CORRESPONDENCE TO THIS P.O. BOX.